Snatches of the overheard conversation sizzled red-hot in Carolyn's brain.

What business was it of Harriet Taylor's—or anyone else's for that matter—if she and Emily stayed single, got married, or joined the circus? Clenching her hands until her well-cared-for nails bit into the palms, Carolyn breathed deeply, glad her niece was absorbed in the service. *Just let Harriet bring on her Herman Dobbs and see what I do to both of them. On the other hand, Emily has managed to send Harriet's motley group of suitors packing.*

So what if Herman Dobbs is already hurrying to Alderdale, seeking a drudge for himself and his five children? Why be concerned? Despite Harriet Taylor and her meddling, that drudge is not going to be Miss Emily Ann Carr.

Carolyn sternly repressed a chuckle at a new thought, a paraphrase of the odious Harriet Taylor, *"Mark my words. Sure as my name is Carolyn Sheffield, I, for one, am not going to let that happen."*

COLLEEN L. REECE was born and raised in a small western Washington logging town. She has written over 130 books and was twice voted **Heartsong Presents'** *Favorite Author of the Year*. Along with her neice **RENEE DEMARCO**, a multi-published, award-winning author and a practicing attorney in Washington State, she has authored many beloved titles.

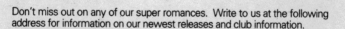

Don't miss out on any of our super romances. Write to us at the following address for information on our newest releases and club information.

Heartsong Presents Readers' Service
PO Box 721
Uhrichsville, OH 44683

Or check out our Web site at www.heartsongpresents.com

Changing
Seasons

For all those who are still waiting for love.

A note from the Author:
We love to hear from our readers! You may correspond with us by writing:

Colleen Reece and Renee DeMarco
Author Relations
PO Box 719
Uhrichsville, OH 44683

ISBN 1-59310-079-5

CHANGING SEASONS

Our mission is to publish and distribute inspirational products offering exceptional value and biblical encouragement to the masses.

prologue

The clump of solid footsteps, the rustle of skirts, and the heavy scent of perfume heralded the first two guests to arrive at Bill Carr's wedding in the small church his family had attended for several generations.

Harriet Taylor—tall, spare, and gimlet-eyed—led the way down the center aisle, leaving her middle-aged daughter a few paces behind, as usual. Harriet's diagonally striped dress gave her all the charm of a black-and-white barber pole. She surveyed the quiet, dimly lit chapel with satisfaction and boomed, "No one here yet. Good. I do like to be first and have my choice of seats." When she reached the reserved area in the front, she ruthlessly tore free the guarding ribbon. "Come, Amelia. We'll sit here. After all, I *am* Bill Carr's third cousin twice removed."

"Yes, Mama." Amelia's subdued voice and demeanor blended with the pale blue outfit Harriet had deemed suitable for one who had lost her husband a year earlier. Amelia's thin shoulders drooped as she preceded Harriet into the pew, the second row from the front. "Shouldn't we sit at the far end, so latecomers can get in more easily?" she timidly asked.

"Nonsense! If people can't arrive on time, it isn't my fault," Harriet snapped.

Amelia's "Yes, Mama" was barely audible.

Harriet planted herself by her daughter, next to the aisle. She peered at the altar and sniffed. "I s'pose Emily brought the flowers from her garden. It's just like her." She scowled at the lovely late-summer roses that tastefully decorated the dimly lighted chapel, drowsing in the afternoon sun. "Seems like she could have forked out for a professional job. After all, Bill *is* her only nephew."

She paused, then pounced on a new topic with both large feet. "I wonder what Emily will do with Bill married and Danielle off to college next week?" When her daughter said nothing, Harriet went on as if there had been no break in her monologue. "You have to hand it to Emily for doing her duty," she offered grudgingly, not bothering to quiet her voice an iota. "I wonder what she'll wear. It's too warm for her old black suit." Harriet sighed as if the weight of the world rested on her sharp-bladed shoulders.

"Maybe she'll wear her lavender crepe," Amelia said. "She looks real nice in it."

"Nice!" Harriet's unladylike snort condemned the garment as being unthinkable. "It's at least five years old and doesn't have an ounce of style." She added condescendingly, "I know the Carrs have had expenses for years, what with all the trouble and such, but a woman owes it to herself to keep from being dowdy. Especially if she ever wants to catch a man." She straightened in the pew and turned to face Amelia. "That's just what Emily needs, you know. A husband. She's going to die an old maid if she keeps on the way she is, just like that aunt of hers, Carolyn Sheffield."

Harriet set her lips in a grim line. "Well, I for one am *not* going to let that happen. One old maid in the family is embarrassing enough, much less two. Carolyn is years beyond help, but I plan to see Emily Carr married off, sure as my name is Harriet Taylor. Or if I can't, it certainly won't be from a lack of trying!"

Amelia's voice rose. "But what more can you do, Mama? You've already sent every Alderdale bachelor and widower from forty to seventy calling. And what good did it do? All

Emily did was smile and tell them her family needed her."

"She doesn't have that excuse any longer," Harriet gloated. "Besides, I know just the person to save Emily from a life of loneliness." She quivered with excitement. "Herman Dobbs—our very own cousin-in-law."

Amelia gasped. *"Herman Dobbs?* He's only thirty-five, ten years younger than Emily!"

Harriet tossed her head. "So much the better. Herman has always been weak, and ever since his waif of a wife died, leaving him with those five children to raise, he's been at his wits' end. It won't be easy for Emily. He doesn't have much in the way of modern conveniences, but she can get by. She's had a lot of practice at doing without. After all, it's not like beggars can be choosers," she added sanctimoniously.

"Shh. People are starting to come in," Amelia warned.

Harriet had the final say. "Mark my words, Amelia. Emily Carr is going to marry Herman Dobbs and be as happy as you and dear Porter were until he died. Herman will do whatever it takes to get himself a wife who will mind the children. He's coming as soon as he possibly can." She leaned back, closed her eyes, and smiled, obviously feeling proud of doing right by "poor Emily."

Her reverie was interrupted by Carolyn Sheffield's voice. "Well, if it isn't Harriet Taylor, spreading warm rays of sunshine, like usual."

With a low moan, Amelia slid as far down in her seat as possible without completely disappearing under the pew in front of them.

Harriet whirled toward the center aisle, indignation deeply etched in every crevice of her thin face. Her mouth flopped open and closed like a brook trout out of water.

Emily Carr, gowned in the scorned lavender crepe, stood silently beside her hopping-mad aunt. Twin spots of scarlet stained her lightly lined face. Although she towered over her stylish sixty-nine-year-old companion, she did not dwarf Carolyn, who was anchored at Harriet's right hand like a 105-pound angel of vengeance.

Harriet Taylor's silence spoke louder than words. Emily could be intimidated; Carolyn could not. Harriet had learned from bitter experience how formidable Emily's aunt could be—especially when it came to her beloved niece.

Now Carolyn's blue eyes looked as if they had been chipped from glaciers. Her voice dripped ice when she said in tones guaranteed to reach all those near enough to have heard Harriet's machinations, "Thank you for your—*concern*, Ms. Taylor. Neither my niece nor I need your matrimonial services." She grasped Emily's arm and led her up to the front row.

"Don't pay any attention to her," Carolyn furiously whispered after they were seated. "Harriet Taylor has always considered herself chief understudy to God. I don't know how she dares set herself up as an authority on marriage! Everyone in Alderdale knows her own marriage was a disaster. Poor Amelia, hitched to Mama Taylor's personally selected 'dear Porter' all those years."

"It's so humiliating," Emily said as her fingers clenched the lavender dress. "She didn't even spare my clothes!" Her fingers stilled. "Bill asked me to wear this."

"You look good and so does the chapel. Bill will love it. Now forget Harriet Taylor and enjoy the wedding," her no-nonsense aunt crisply advised. "*I* intend to." She resettled herself in her seat, raised her chin, and crossed her arms in the way that always made Emily smile.

It worked. By the time Bill followed the minister out of a side room and gave Emily a crooked I-love-you grin, Harriet Taylor and her plotting might as well have been dead and buried in the Pacific Ocean.

&

Not so for Carolyn. Her mind running double track between the wedding and Harriet Taylor, Carolyn squared her shoulders and clenched her jaw. Good thing she had canceled an important business appointment and driven down from Seattle this morning. The more she thought about the incident, the angrier she grew. At least her years of experience as a professional paralegal had taught her the value of concealing her feelings. What Emily needed was support, not a display of rage. Besides, it was illegal for a sixty-nine-year-old woman to leave her seat and throttle a meddler, especially in the middle of her great-nephew's wedding.

Snatches of the overheard conversation sizzled red-hot in Carolyn's brain. What business was it of Harriet Taylor's—or anyone else's for that matter—if she and Emily stayed single, got married, or joined the circus? Clenching her hands until her well-cared-for nails bit into the palms, Carolyn breathed deeply, glad her niece was absorbed in the service. *Just let Harriet bring on her Herman Dobbs and see what I do to both of them. On the other hand, Emily has managed to send Harriet's motley group of suitors packing.*

So what if Herman Dobbs is already hurrying to Alderdale, seeking a drudge for himself and his five children? Why be concerned? Despite Harriet Taylor and her meddling, that drudge is not going to be Miss Emily Ann Carr.

Carolyn sternly repressed a chuckle at a new thought, a paraphrase of the odious Harriet Taylor, *"Mark my words. Sure as my name is Carolyn Sheffield, I, for one, am not going to let that happen."*

Part 1: Emily

one

Approximately fifty miles southwest of Portland, Oregon, the winds of change crested the Coast Range. They gathered momentum with every mile. When they reached Alderdale—the small town that looked as if it had been lifted from a Norman Rockwell painting and set down in the Oregon forest—the breezes shooed away lingering wisps of fog and gleefully moved on. The inhabitants of Alderdale were left to enjoy a perfect day.

From her seat near an open window in the inner office of the Gerard & Son law firm, Alderdale's largest because of the "& Son," Emily Carr breathed in the fresh air, then watched swaying tree branches slowly return to their usual position. Would she also slowly settle back into her usual position? *Never,* she vowed. She unclenched tightly-clasped fingers, glad the elder Gerard had been called away for a few moments. It gave her time to try and assimilate what she'd just learned. The winds of change that still blew through Gerard & Son's office, sparked hope.

Snatches of a poem Emily learned as a young girl came to mind. The poem described a road that lured the adventurous west, east, south, and north. While most roads led homeward, this road encouraged readers to "leave gray miles behind" and travel "in quest of that one beauty God put me here to find."

"West, east, south, and north," Emily softly repeated. She bowed her head and closed her eyes. Visions of cities and seas, mountains and valleys, burning desert sands and icy glaciers kaleidoscoped through her mind. Her heart pounded. Had the long-delayed "someday," for which her longing heart clung to during all the gray miles her sensible shoes had traveled, really come?

"Heavenly Father, my roads so far all have led homeward. Have You really opened a way for me to seek Your beauty? If so, what is the beauty I am to find?"

Her answer was a burst of song from a bird in the large maple tree just outside the office window. Emily opened her eyes and located the soloist: a little brown bird that clung to the highest swaying branch. How amazing for glorious music to spring from just a tiny bunch of feathers! Emily smiled in empathy with the plain little songster. She also had no fine feathers—just a heart filled with songs yet to be sung.

I wonder what Aunt Carolyn will say about my good news?

The unspoken words brought a familiar twinge. Emily loved and admired her only aunt but always felt awed by her presence. *Why?* she wondered for the thousandth time. It certainly wasn't size. Emily's nervousness fled and a chuckle broke the silence. She towered over Carolyn Sheffield by a good six inches and outweighed her plain-speaking aunt by twenty-five pounds.

Perhaps it was the age difference—the fact go-getter Carolyn was twenty-four when Emily was born, well on her way toward making a mark in her chosen career. She hadn't had much time for Emily or her brother Davey, born five years after Emily, although they always recognized that she was fond of them.

"If things had been different, I might have been more like her," Emily mused. She sighed and shook her head. Life had marked out vastly different paths for each of them. Their only similarity was in sacrificing their chances for love and giving themselves to a purpose instead. *Carolyn's sacrifice was from choice,* a little voice whispered in Emily's soul. *Yours was out of necessity.*

Emily impatiently squelched the inner voice. No use reliving her childish determination to "take care of Dad and Davey" after her mother died when Emily was ten. Or the long, weary years of her father's invalidism, which required all of Emily's faith and strength to care for him after his logging accident.

Pain too deep for tears stabbed at her heart and she unseeingly stared into the early summer day. "Why, God?" she said. "Mama. Daddy. Davey." *David,* she reminded herself. The name *Davey* belonged to the child her beloved brother had once been, to a happier time with the little brother she'd cared for and played with. It didn't fit the stony-faced man who, after the departure of his dissatisfied wife, pleaded with his sister to care for his small children. Neither did it fit the forty-year-old Captain David Carr, who had given his life for his country while serving in the Middle East, leaving his children fatherless.

Emily forced her mind away from the past when Isaiah Gerard, senior member of the firm, reappeared and strode to the worn office chair his wife had long since given up threatening to abolish. He sank his ample, white-haired bulk into its depths. His keen dark eyes twinkled. "Emily Ann Carr, if anyone deserves to fall into good fortune, it is you." He waxed eloquent on a subject obviously dear to his heart. "When I think of you being tied down for. . .how long has it been?"

Emily struggled to regain her composure. In three decades, no one except Isaiah had ever called her Emily Ann. It made her feel like a young girl—the girl that life had jealously kept her from being. "Thirty-five years." She paused. "My family needed me." She proudly raised her head. "I don't regret it."

Isaiah grunted. "You wouldn't, being you." He fumbled for a handkerchief in his rumpled jacket and loudly blew his nose. "Back to business. Who would have thought, after all this time, that what was considered worthless stock in your daddy's friend's mine would prove valuable?"

He didn't wait for an answer but gestured toward the open window that framed an incomparable view of a bald eagle ascribing circles in the blue sky. "So, what are you going to do now that you're free as that fella?"

Emily felt a tingle of new life and opening vistas stir within her like fluttering wings. "I had no idea why you asked me to stop by. We've always had to live frugally. Now. . ."

"You won't be rich, but there's enough to keep you comfortable, no matter what the economy does," Isaiah promised. He cocked his shaggy head to one side. "Emily Ann, can't you think of *anything* you want to do?"

The wings took flight. A cry, born from her years of restrictions, burst out, magnified by Harriet Taylor's critical comments on the way she dressed. "Yes. I will throw away every piece of 'sensible' clothing I own and go shopping in Portland!"

Isaiah Gerard looked at Emily as if she had taken leave of her senses. Perhaps she had. If she'd had time to think, it was *not* the answer she'd have given. The utter look of shock on Isaiah's face accomplished what Harriet's careless remark had started weeks earlier. Emily felt gales of laughter rise within her. She clutched the arms of her chair and let it pour into the room. Laughter, absent for too much of her life. Laughter, coming when tears would not. Cleansing, healing laughter that changed to tears.

Isaiah handed her a box of tissues and let her cry.

At last the storm subsided. Emily gulped, blew her nose, and stammered, "Forgive me. I. . ."

"No apologies, Emily Ann. Best thing in the world for you," the old lawyer told her gruffly. He pointed to a door that she knew from previous visits led directly into a private washroom. "Go mop your face. Then we'll talk."

She choked back a final sob and did his bidding, splashing cold water into her face again and again. When she raised her head and caught sight of herself in the washroom mirror, she gasped. A blue sparkle had replaced her tears. The peace of one who has fought a good fight and conquered had subtracted years from her countenance. Even the few glints of silver in her disarrayed brown hair shone like tiny mountain streams threading their way to the valleys below. Gratefulness flooded her body. "Thank You, God," she whispered.

Emily opened the washroom door, switched off the light, squared her shoulders, and walked out of the shadows into the sunlit office.

two

To the inhabitants of Alderdale, the Emily Ann Carr who left the law firm of Gerard & Son looked no different from the well-known woman who had walked the tree-lined streets earlier that day.

Emily knew better. Although she smiled, nodded to acquaintances, and returned pleasant greetings, her heart kept time with the music in her soul. Music punctuated with the sweet sounds of loosening shackles and breaking chains.

The perfect day shimmered around Emily, as rich with hope as a rainbow after a storm. She pinched her arm to make sure it wasn't just a lovely dream, a fleeting moment that would soon be overcome by reality. The sharp nip of her fingers reassured her. The music of freedom gloriously proclaimed the joyous news that her long-awaited "someday" had arrived.

Someday. How she had clung to its promise through all the years of fulfilling her vow to "take care of Daddy and Davey." Someday she would be able to think of herself. Someday wonderful things would happen. Someday her prayers and dreams would come true. Psalm 37:4 had become her watchword in the darkest hours: "Delight thyself also in the LORD; and He shall give thee the desires of thine heart." So she gladly served, trusted her heavenly Father. . .and waited.

Emily wanted to skip, to shout, to laugh. She nobly restrained herself. Such behavior would set the local gossips, especially Harriet Taylor, buzzing like a swarm of angry hornets. A chuckle escaped in spite of her determination to act as usual. She muffled it in a spotless handkerchief and turned in at the gate of the old Carr place.

How shabby it looked, the two-story white house built when Alderdale first came into existence! A pang went through Emily. In her great-grandparents' day, it had been one of the finest homes in town. Now it reminded her of an ancient, but well-loved, family dog—cherished because of long association, not beauty. Or a dowager in faded finery, gathering her skirts around her in an attempt to maintain dignity. Even though Emily had been able to keep up major repairs, the house badly needed painting, and a new roof would do wonders for its appearance.

She slowly walked up the path leading from the picket fence to the wide covered porch. Pink, red, yellow, and white roses clambered up the porch posts and perfumed the air with memories. She dropped into the porch swing that had hung there since she was a child. Sister Feline, the black-and-white cat Danielle—Emily's niece—had found as a kitten and mischievously named because her markings resembled a nun's habit, curled up in Emily's lap. "We'll pronounce it *Feh-leen*," Danielle had gleefully announced. "It's more elegant than Fe-line, and still means 'cat.' "

Emily smiled at the memory. Shabby or not, this was home. "Even if I decide to travel, I'll keep the house," Emily told her cat. "I can afford to fix it up. That way I'll always have a place to come home to when I grow tired of wandering." Sister Feline's gravelly purr gave no argument.

Emily started the porch swing gently rocking. The motion, combined with the cat's companionship, calmed her as nothing else could have done. She bowed her head. "Heavenly Father, it's the strangest feeling. The past is over, but the future is so uncertain, it's almost frightening. I'm like the old woman traveling on the king's highway who wondered if she were really herself, and if not, who she could be. I certainly don't feel like myself."

Her thoughts trailed off and she closed her eyes. A jumble

of memories and things to consider immediately assailed her, clamoring for her attention. The habit of years when she could only find stolen moments for reflection also plagued her, along with the feeling that she needed to be up and doing something. Anything.

She finally realized what was bothering her. "I need time to think," she told Sister Feline. "I have to make the transition from the person I was, to the one I will be." She drew in a deep breath. "There is only one way." Setting the cat on the porch floor, Emily opened the screen door. The narrow hall—with its staircase to the upper-level living room on one side, dining room and kitchen on the other—felt cool after being outdoors. It was cool and fragrant from furniture polish and the bouquet of roses Emily had picked and placed on the hall table just before receiving the summons to the law office. That seemed an eternity ago, not just a few earth-shaking hours.

After consuming a cup of herbal tea and a sandwich at the round dining-room table that had hosted countless family gatherings, Emily went to her bedroom. A well-fed Sister Feline followed. Emily turned the key of the foot locker in her large closet and removed a great stack of notebooks. "These aren't for you," she warned the cat, whose reaching paw and inquisitive nose indicated a tendency to investigate. Sister Feline meowed and trailed Emily to the living room. With no lap invitation forthcoming from her mistress, who was seated on the worn but comfortable couch amidst a clutter of notebooks, the cat plumped down on the hearth rug and began to groom herself.

No one but Emily and God knew the "Secret of the Notebooks." She had named them that at age ten, when she first began filling the pages in a desperate attempt to hide her grief from her father and little brother, lest it make them feel even worse. The books were not diaries—neat little blank volumes offering a few lines on which to record daily events—but fat journals. From the time her mother died, Emily poured her innermost soul into her writing. Joy and sorrow. Letters to God when she could not put the prayers of her heart into words. Feelings of comfort and peace that never failed to follow such entries. All these were mingled with stories she wrote to amuse young Davey. Thirty-five years, starting with pencil recordings in composition books that gave way to neat ink entries in bound blank journals. A review of her life to date.

"I haven't read these journals in years." Emily whispered so quietly that Sister Feline only flicked an ear in her direction and went on washing. "I know it won't be easy, but it's necessary to reconcile with the past before I can move into the future." She opened the first notebook and began to read. Tears came unbidden with the first childishly formed words:

My Journal
by Emily Ann Carr, age 10

Mama went to heaven today. I feel sad.

The words on the page blurred. A scene swept into Emily's mind, a scene as vivid as the day her mother died. Mama's long illness had stolen her strength, but it hadn't diminished her faith and loving spirit. Emily could almost feel her mother's transparent hand on hers when she said, "Emily Ann, I want you to know what a comfort you are to me. You are Daddy's and my own beloved daughter." Her eyes sparkled as they hadn't done in a long time. "You are also a wonderful sister to little Davey. I've seen the way he follows you like a shadow."

A smile softened the sharp planes of her thin face. "Knowing he and Daddy will still have you when I'm gone brings me peace. You have learned your lessons well, my child. Young as you are, you're already a better cook and housekeeper than most of the women and girls in Alderdale. I am very proud of you."

Emily didn't fully understand what her mother meant at the time. Long years passed before she recognized the truth. Mama hadn't been laying the burden of looking after father and brother on Emily's slim shoulders. She had been offering the only consolation she had left to give—pride in her daughter, a memory to lighten the pain of parting. She never dreamed her praise would unknowingly light a candle of resolve in Emily's childish heart: *Daddy and Davey need me. I will take care of them.*

The memories rushed on.

Davey asking, "Mama, will you forget me?"

Mama, smiling through her tears. "I could never forget my little boy, or Daddy, or Emily Ann. Be a good boy, Davey. Do what Daddy and sister tell you. Grow up to be a strong man who loves God. Someday we will all be together again. Now, give me a hug and a kiss, and go out under the big tree. You, too, Emily Ann."

Mama's hug and whisper, "Always remember the peace you gave me."

Davey's grubby hand in Emily's as they sat beneath the tree by the fence.

Daddy, coming from the house with his arms outstretched. Emily knew Mama had gone to heaven even before he had told them.

Finally, the memory of tightening her arms around her father and little brother, silently repeating her vow: *Daddy and Davey need me. I will take care of them.*

Emily dropped the notebook to her lap. Scorching tears fell. How well she remembered that long-ago day and the bewildering weeks that followed!

She continued reading. The meager journal entries, as if the writer had no time or heart for writing, bore mute witness to the loss of the beloved mother. Occasional golden sentences stood out like shafts of light in the family's dark world. Davey's finding a buttercup and laughing when Emily held it under her chin so that it made her skin look yellow. Davey's sixth birthday.

Again Emily had to stop. She felt a chuckle rise in her throat. She had reminded her father it was Davey's birthday. He brought a cake mix and birthday candles from the store. Davey said it was the "bestest cake in the whole world," even though the frosting stayed runny. It made her father laugh, the first time in months.

It was a long while before Emily could take up the notebook and go on. The turning of dog-eared, yellowed pages whispered down the long path from the past and into the silent room. Sister Feline yawned, curled into a ball, and relaxed into sleep.

A succession of much-later entries followed. Emily skimmed them, sometimes rereading certain passages. Now and then, she paused to unfold time-worn, creased pieces of paper tucked between the pages: poetry and quotations. She hadn't remembered how strong her childhood dreams were all those years ago.

> *Someday I will write wonderful stories and see faraway lands. Someday I will buy Davey things he doesn't ask for. He knows it would make Daddy feel bad that we can't afford them.*
> *Someday I will do things for others. Daddy says I already have—for him and Davey. Mama, if you can see me, you know I'm taking care of them.*

Emily paused to marvel at the child she had been. Even though the confident expectation dwindled a bit, and a degree of resignation crept into the journal entries as the years passed, the shining hope for "someday" continued.

Emily returned to her task. She relived the tragic logging accident that left her father an invalid and more dependent on her than ever. Unwilling to dwell on the shattering time period, Emily laid the journal aside and moved to another.

She lingered over some of the entries from her early teen years. A tender smile curled her lips.

I am so excited! I've been promoted to the Advanced Language Arts class! I'm the youngest person in class and will have to work hard to keep up. I don't mind.

Some of my classmates don't act very pleased at having me with them. One boy is really nice, though. He is two years older than I am and has dark hair, a wide smile, and twinkling dark eyes. His name is Nathan Hamilton. I looked his name up in a book that tells about names. Nathan means "gift."

Our teacher, Mrs. Sorenson, had us write an essay. Nathan said his dream is to be a writer. I've never told anyone, but that's what I want to be, too. I wish the stories I write and tell Davey were as good as Nathan's stories. At least I'm a good speller. Nathan isn't. He's always asking me how to spell "atavistic" or "precocious," or some other big word Mrs. Sorenson says is pretentious.

Nathan is polite, but he doesn't pay much attention to girls. He's too busy writing and studying and playing sports.

He always acts like he appreciates it when I help him. His dark eyes laugh. Well, not really. Mrs. Sorenson keeps reminding us that eyes can't laugh or fall to the ground, or do any of those things some books say they do. She tells us to say "gaze," as in, "Her gaze fell to the ground," but it doesn't sound right to say "His dark gaze laughs."

Nathan is the only one except Mr. Gerard, the lawyer (and he doesn't count), who calls me "Em'ly Ann," as if both names run together. I feel like a different person when Nathan whispers, "Em'ly Ann, how do you spell 'atrocious'? My a-t-r-o-s-h-u-s doesn't look right." Then he grins.

Nathan is always quoting from Walden, *by Henry David Thoreau: "If a man does not keep pace with his companions perhaps it is because he hears a different drummer. Let him step to the music which he hears, however measured or far away." It sends chills chasing up and down my spine.*

Nathan hears that music, the beat of a different drum. I can tell by the way he speaks the words and the way his eyes glisten. I hear it, too.

Someday I will be free to follow the different drumbeat. I wonder if either of us will ever become an author. I am going to try. I want to write stories that will help to make the world a better place. Is it unrealistic to hope they will be published? No one from Alderdale has ever been published, except in the local newspaper.

I know it won't be easy. Matthew 22:14 says, "For many are called, but few are chosen." Will Nathan be chosen? Will I?

A plaintive "meow" from Sister Feline bridged the gap between junior high days and the present. Emily roused to discover that dusk lurked just outside the windows. Lengthening shadows surrounded her. Still under the spell cast by her mental journey to the past, Emily laid aside the journal and made room on her lap for the cat. She switched on a nearby lamp, leaving the rest of the living room in partial darkness.

Whatever happened to Nathan Hamilton? Did he ever think of the shy girl who used to help him with his spelling? More important, had he been able to fulfill *his* dream? At the end of the school term, he and his family had moved. Not even Harriet Taylor had been able to ferret out their whereabouts.

Emily sighed. For years she had searched *Books in Print*. No Nathan or Nate Hamilton was ever listed. Evidently his boyhood dream had been derailed, as hers had been. He would be forty-seven now. If Nathan had carried through with his plans, surely he would be published. Emily sadly shook her head. What a waste. Even the strict, impossible-to-please language arts teacher had admitted Nathan had talent. Mrs. Sorenson had been harder on Nathan and Emily than on anyone else in the class. On the rare occasions when she praised their work, they exchanged glances of delight.

On the last day of school, their teacher had called them aside and announced in her usual brusque manner, "You both have writing ability. That's why I pushed you. I've done all I can. Now what you do with your God-given talent is out of my hands."

If only Mrs. Sorenson had stayed in Alderdale, instead of transferring to another school at the end of the term, Emily thought while preparing for bed. In spite of all the obligations to Daddy and Davey, perhaps things would have been different.

If only Nathan had stayed in Alderdale, her heart whispered, *perhaps things would have been even more different.*

Emily felt hot color flood her face. The "Secret of the Notebooks" wasn't the only buried secret in her life. All through the years, whenever she thought of the mate she felt God intended her to have, a crystal-clear image rose from her heart to her mind. Tall and strong, straight as a mountain fir, as filled with joy as the streams that laughed their way to the sea, her "someday" love was simply a grown-up edition of Nathan Hamilton.

three

Tired without being sleepy, Emily propped herself up in bed in the pale green and white bedroom that had been hers since childhood. The walls could use a fresh coat of paint; now they could have it.

Emily smiled and continued reading her journals. The digital clock on her bookcase headboard showed 4:30 before she finished the last one. Sister Feline lay curled at the foot of the bed. *Is she dreaming dreams of her own?* Emily wondered.

A cool breeze stirred the simple white window curtains, then danced across the quiet room, out the open door, and into the upstairs hall. An early-rising bird caroled a single, day-welcoming note. It began a chorus in the trees outside the window.

A searching sunbeam discovered and touched Emily's face. She felt as if she had returned from a very long journey. Her life events, so faithfully and poignantly recorded in her journals, fell into formation and again marched through her mind:

Her injured father's long illness and his unwillingness to allow anyone except his daughter to care for him, even though it meant Emily could not attend college.

The continuing need to stretch a disability income to meet the needs of three people.

Mr. Carr's prideful refusal to accept offers of help from his wife's sister, Carolyn Sheffield.

His death many years later.

The expectation of release from duty and the opportunity for Emily to have a life of her own.

The desertion of her military brother, David Carr, and his two small children, Bill and Danielle, by his wife.

The further postponement of Emily's dream in order to help where needed.

The death, somewhere in the Middle East, of the brother she loved.

The task of comforting David's grieving children as Emily had once comforted Davey.

The humiliation of being called an old maid.

Harriet Taylor's never-ending stream of impossible suitors.

Emily's admiration for Aunt Carolyn, busily making a mark in her chosen career.

Emily's reward when Bill and Danielle credited her with their honors and success.

The sacrifices of education, fashionable clothing, travel, *even love,* for the sake of the children who thought of her as their real mother.

The years she served as a caregiver—until Bill married and Danielle won a full scholarship to a prestigious eastern university.

A quiet house with only Sister Feline for company.

Finally, the stunning revelation—not yet fully registered in her mind—that opened the way for Emily to do all the things she'd dreamed of doing. . .for what felt like forever.

Would they include love? Emily turned off her bed light and pondered, while the walls of her room gathered color from the coming day. So many journal entries had to do with her desire for love. Not just love of family and God, but the love of a good man, one to whom she could joyously repeat the timeless words Ruth spoke to her mother-in-law, Naomi, in the Bible: "Intreat me not to leave thee, or to return from following after thee: for whither thou goest, I will go; and where thou lodgest, I will lodge: thy people shall be my people, and thy God my God."

For a single moment, Emily's strong faith faltered. "Lord, what if I am too old for love?" she whispered into her line-dried pillowcase. Then, "No! I've waited all these years. I can't bear living the rest of my life alone, the target of Harriet Taylor's cruel taunts and everlasting matchmaking."

Emily's protest awakened Sister Feline. She leaped from the bed and disappeared out the open bedroom door in a streak of black and white.

Filled with rebellion at the possible loss of her most treasured dream, Emily ignored the abrupt departure and stared out the window into the blue heavens. "I'm neither Cinderella nor Sleeping Beauty, Lord, but now that I'm free, surely love will come. I don't want a knight in shining armor. Or a prince on a white horse. Just someone who serves You, and who will love, honor, and cherish me."

Exhausted more by her emotions than the sleepless night, Emily closed her eyes and waited for peace to steal into her troubled heart and mind. Halfway between sleep and awareness, visions of Nathan Hamilton's twinkling dark eyes, wide grin, and fondness for many-syllable words, swirled through Emily's mind. Her last waking thought was: *Nathan will never know how intensely I shared his love for writing—just that Mrs. Sorenson said I had talent. He will never know the joy and brightness he brought into my dull life. I wish. . .* Sleep claimed her before she could finish her thought.

❧

Emily Ann Carr awakened on a morning that Alderdale considered just another in a series of late summer days. She knew the day began a new era for her. A favorite Scripture, Psalm 118:24, came to mind: "This is the day which the LORD hath made; we will rejoice and be glad in it."

Emily was far too happy to contain her feelings. She sang the praise song taken from the ancient Scripture, ably accompanied by Sister Feline's rumbling alto purr. After breakfast, she whipped through her morning chores and prepared to go out.

A goodly sum of money lay in the bottom of her plain purse. The largest balance she'd ever possessed fattened her normally lean checkbook. Emily quickly concealed a few "egg basket" bills inside her clothing, recalling a story about Grandmother Sheffield. When Aunt Carolyn was a child, her mother lost her handbag while shopping in Portland. "What are we going to do?" a worried Carolyn asked.

"Now, don't you concern yourself," Grandmother Sheffield admonished. "I don't carry all my eggs in one basket." She led the way to an empty restroom nearby, where she unfastened the garter holding up her long cotton sock and removed a ten-dollar bill. From then on, the Sheffield family motto was, "Don't carry all your eggs in one basket."

"I wonder if Aunt Carolyn still stashes cash." Emily laughed. She found it hard to imagine anyone attempting to steal anything from Ms. Carolyn Sheffield! Aunt Carolyn marched through life with a don't-mess-with-me-or-else stride that gave an impression of added height. When necessary, her blue eyes could don an icy stare, a stare guaranteed to humble her adversaries.

Emily closed her front and screen doors and set off on foot for the downtown bus station. The desire to skip her way down Main Street that had pestered her the day before, returned. Even those in the early autumn of their lives should pay tribute to good fortune. Emily allowed herself one childish skip, under the guise of avoiding a rough spot in the sidewalk. A smile started in her heart. It crept up and erupted into a laugh. What fun to have a secret in a town where secrets didn't remain secrets for long.

"Not so this time," she gloated. "Isaiah Gerard is as close-mouthed as a razor clam. Even Harriet Taylor won't be able to pry anything out of him."

"Emily Carr, you look like the cat that gobbled the canary," a familiar voice accused. "What are you mumbling about?"

Speak of the devil, and her horns appear. Emily silently chastised herself for the uncharacteristically uncharitable thought and said amiably, "Hello, Harriet. It certainly is a nice day."

Harriet barely glanced at the sunny sky before turning back to Emily. Avid curiosity shone in her searching gaze, and she looked more like a barber pole than ever in the red-and-white striped dress that hung loosely on her angular frame. "So, what did Isaiah Gerard want? I hear he called you in."

"I really can't say," Emily said, using the ploy she'd discovered worked well with nosy people. It allowed her to remain truthful without explaining whether she couldn't say because she didn't know, or because she wasn't at liberty to divulge information.

Harriet's mouth flew open, but no words fell out.

Emily took advantage of her tormentor's speechlessness and remarked, "I really have to be running along if I'm to catch the bus. Do have a pleasant day."

She made her escape, followed by an indignant gasp and Harriet's comment, "Well, I never! What's gotten into you, Emily Carr?"

Gleeful at her adroit handling of her long-time tormentor, Emily hurried away before Harriet could gather her wits and ask where she was going and why.

❧

The bus ride from Alderdale to Portland gave Emily a little over an hour to make a list. The shopping mall she and Danielle patronized on their trips to the city had a variety of department stores. Several offered quality clothing at reasonable prices. Despite Isaiah Gerard's assurance that she need never scrimp again, Emily did not intend to go overboard in assembling her new wardrobe.

It was a spree to remember. Emily selected clothing to satisfy her beauty-starved soul. Modest and well-cut, nothing outlandish. She bypassed dark and serviceable garments, concentrating on soft blues, greens, rose, cream, and white. Even the house dresses she chose were bright and pretty. A navy suit she admired came with a gorgeous scarlet scarf. Should she. . . ? Well, why not? If Harriet Taylor could dress herself in red-striped dresses, surely Emily Carr could add pizzazz with a red silk scarf.

On her way to the cashier, a tastefully displayed dress caught her attention. A lavender dress cut along the same lines as the tired gown Emily now wore. But what a difference! The beautifully tailored garment boasted a lace collar and impeccable workmanship. The desire to own it surged through Emily. What better way to silently rebuke Harriet Taylor for her unkind comments than by showing up at church wearing an exquisite replica of the dress Harriet had scorned.

The dress fit perfectly, but was far more costly than any of the others Emily had chosen. *Take it,* she fiercely told herself. *You deserve this dress and everything else you're buying.* She slipped into her old dress and carried the lavender dress to the cashier.

"Do you want these shipped?" the saleswoman asked.

"All but this one." Emily pointed to her final selection. "I need shoes to go with it."

It didn't take long to find a pair of soft gray shoes that complemented the dress. Emily treated herself to chicken salad and a tall, cool glass of lemonade in a quiet tea room, then purchased a leather-bound journal before catching the bus to Alderdale.

❧

Sunday dawned bright and clear. Emily ate breakfast, fed her cat, and put on the lavender dress. She peered into her mirror. What a difference new clothing made! She looked and felt years younger. She walked to church and quietly entered. Harriet Taylor and her daughter, Amelia, stood just inside the door. Amelia's plain face blossomed into a smile that made her almost pretty. Harriet's did not. Her disbelieving expression was worth every penny Emily had invested in the lavender dress!

Following several announcements and the usual songfest, the minister said, "Our text this morning is Mark 2:21: 'No man also seweth a piece of new cloth on an old garment. . . .'"

A choking sound from Harriet's direction nearly proved Emily's undoing. Was the choosing of that particular Scripture pure coincidence? Or did God have a sense of humor the size of the highest peak in the Coast Range? It took all of Emily's self-control to maintain proper decorum and force her mind back to the sermon.

Late that afternoon, while Sister Feline drowsed on a sunny windowsill, Emily opened the journal she had purchased as a symbol of new beginnings. She dated the first page with the date she'd gone to see Isaiah Gerard, then recorded the events of the past few days. She finished her entry with:

> *Perhaps it was wrong of me to get so much enjoyment from the shock on Harriet Taylor's face. It's just that. . .*

Emily's pen faltered. The memory of the befuddled woman's countenance floated between her and her journal. She brushed it aside and quickly wrote:

> *Lord, none of this good fortune is my doing. Help me remember it is a gift from You. Thank You.*

&

By the end of the week, Harriet's, "Well, I never! What's gotten into Emily Carr?" had spread through Alderdale like a river in flood. Harriet repeated it so often and to so many people, Isaiah Gerard sourly stated the day of the Town Crier hadn't passed.

Speculation about Emily's new clothes reached fever pitch. They weren't Carolyn Sheffield's castoffs, everyone agreed. They were obviously new. Besides, the two women could never wear the same size.

Emily kept her own counsel. The news of her change in circumstances would eventually become public knowledge. At least Herman Dobbs hadn't yet shown up. According to the local grapevine, his youngest child had broken his arm. Emily pitied the boy but thanked God for the postponement of an unpleasant, Harriet Taylor–inspired interview. With prayer and trepidation, she took a bold step toward doing something entirely for herself, something she had longed to do ever since she made up stories to entertain her little brother. She enrolled in a hands-on writing class at a nearby Christian college. She knew it wouldn't be easy. She dreaded having to read her work before strangers even more now than she had in the Advanced Language Arts class.

To Emily's great relief, the instructor announced at the first class, "I have few rules, but they are to be strictly observed. Constructive criticism is always welcome. Negative comments will not be tolerated." He outlined the contents of the course and ended with, "There is no better way to perfect our writing than by reading the work of authors we admire. Your next assignment is to choose a contemporary novel, preferably one you have read more than once, and write a letter to the author. Tell him or her how and why the book spoke to you."

He scowled. "Please, people, spare me the platitudes and generalities. Go beyond the obvious and look for hidden treasure. Try to crawl inside the author's skin and see what motivation led to the title you choose. Then write your letter. It doesn't matter whether you receive an answer. Some of you won't. What counts is your having identified the elements of good writing and how they have been applied."

Emily drove home in a state of near panic. Had signing up for the class been a terrible mistake? Who was she to write such a letter? "Stop it," she ordered herself. "Remember what Henry Ford said? 'Obstacles are those frightful things you see when you take your eyes off your goal.'" The admonition brought comfort. Long before she reached Alderdale, Emily had mentally inventoried her bookshelves and chosen a book and author. Her light burned into the early morning hours as she reread a title that had made a difference in her life.

The next day, Herman Dobbs and his five stair-step children appeared on her doorstep. He pushed his way into the hall and wasted no time in speaking his piece. "Miss Emily, it's been brought to my attention that you are no longer tied down and that you are interested in having a home and family of your own. I'm here today to offer you my hand and my heart." A huge paw slapped the middle of his chest. "We can either live here, or. . ."

"Pardon me, Mr. Dobbs," Emily interrupted in an icy voice worthy even of Aunt Carolyn. "You have been grossly misinformed concerning my circumstances. I am not interested in receiving either your hand or your heart."

The stolid man blinked. "You refuse to take pity on these five motherless children?" he demanded, pointing at the cluster of urchins balefully eyeing Emily from outside the screen door. If their expressions accurately indicated their feelings about having Emily Carr as a new mother, they were even less eager than she for her to assume such a role!

Herman Dobbs wasn't through. He pointed a fat finger at her and demanded, "How can a good Christian woman such as you are said to be, fail to have mercy on a poor, lonely man trying to raise five motherless children?"

The whole scene was so like a scene from an old-time melodrama, Emily struggled to keep from laughing, in spite of her indignation. She had dealt with previous matrimonial candidates according to their varied approaches, but never had she encountered the effrontery Herman Dobbs displayed! She disciplined the beginnings of a smile that might convey to him that she was weakening, then primly said, "God has not put it into my heart to care for either you or your motherless children, Mr. Dobbs. Good day."

She shooed the protesting man onto the porch, went inside, and locked her door, to the tune of loud thumps and Herman calling, "Beggars can't afford to be choosers, Miss Carr. I will call again!" He sounded so much like his cousin-in-law, Harriet, that Emily felt like going upstairs and dumping a bucket of water down on his conceited head.

A few days later, news of her inheritance leaked out. According to hearsay, the amount ranged between $25,000 and $2,000,000. "Let 'em think what they wish," Isaiah Gerard advised Emily when she dropped by his office. "They will, anyway. I don't know who got the information, but I suspect one of our phone conversations was overheard."

Emily sighed. "I've already begun receiving letters begging for money."

The lawyer shook his shaggy white head. "Don't let it get you down, Em'ly Ann. 'This, too, shall pass.'" His eyes twinkled.

She laughed in spite of her annoyance. "The sooner, the better!"

Emily wasn't laughing when she got home. Five screaming Dobbs children swarmed through her yard. Harriet Taylor and Herman Dobbs, who had obviously been hanging around waiting for Emily to change her mind, were parked on the Carr front porch. They must have hot-footed it to the Carr home the moment news of Emily's inheritance reached their greedy ears.

"Dear Emily," Harriet gushed, "we are *so* happy for you! Is it really true you are now the richest person in town?"

Emily brushed past her. "You'll have to excuse me, Harriet. I have a headache." She opened the screen door, barely missing Herman Dobbs's nose.

She *did* have a headache. Seven of them, in fact, cluttering up her front porch, her yard—and if Harriet Taylor could manage it, the rest of Emily Ann Carr's life.

four

Nathan Hamilton, a.k.a. *N. Alexander*—his first initial and middle name—dropped the pen he'd been using to proof his latest novel and flexed cramped fingers. Just a few pages to go. Good. *The Overcomer* was his most satisfying project to date. It had also been his most challenging. The army of loyal fans who had flocked to buy *The Seeker* a year earlier had sent sales skyrocketing, placing the title at the top of both Christian and secular best-seller lists. Readers and reviewers demanded a sequel.

Would *The Overcomer* find an equally responsive audience? God grant that it would. Nate's protagonist represented all who meet life's bitterness in their search for peace in a chaotic world. People needed to be reminded of the simple truth Jesus promised in John 14:1, as Nate's overcomer had done: "Do not let your hearts be troubled. Trust in God; trust also in me."

With a prayer that the book would be instrumental in bringing peace, if only to the hearts of individuals, Nate picked up his pen, impatient to finish and get outside into the fresh September morning. He yawned and glanced through the window of the apartment he'd inhabited for the past several months. Except for the persistent sunlight making tunnels in San Francisco's early-morning fog, his accommodations were similar to dozens of others he'd had. New York, Toronto, Mexico City, Tokyo—none was ever a home, simply a place to research, write with few interruptions, and revise until Nate knew it was time to let go and submit his manuscript.

He chuckled, remembering the question invariably asked during interviews the world around. "Tell us, Mr. Alexander. What is your finest novel?"

His quick reply, "My next," always brought a wave of surprise and the need to explain. "Authors should strive to make every project better than the last. 'Just as good as' isn't acceptable."

Nathan stretched to his full height and went back to his job. A few minor comments, a protest against an editorial change that lessened the impact of what he wanted to express, and *The Overcomer* was finished. The bone-weary author knew he was too keyed-up to sleep. He needed physical exercise to counterbalance the stimulus of reliving the just-proofed book, so he ran through a list of possible places to spend the day.

Nate had long since developed the habit of talking to himself. He'd found the sound of his voice was better than too much silence. Now he told his growling stomach, "Fisherman's Wharf first. Seafood chowder, sourdough bread, coleslaw, and salty air are just what I need." He grabbed a windbreaker, opted for the stairs rather than the elevator, and headed down to the street. A pang went through him. Too bad he didn't have someone with whom to enjoy this incomparable day. Someone to join him on the cable cars, explore Chinatown, or visit Golden Gate Park.

"The motto 'He travels fastest who travels alone' isn't as wonderful as people think," Nate complained. He thought of the struggling years he'd spent trying to break into the Christian fiction market, long before the genre exploded into its present popularity. It had been necessary to follow assignments wherever they took him. Things didn't change much with his first successful title, despite his being hounded by publishers and the public clamoring for more books.

"According to the press, people envy me because I've remained single and able to roam the world," Nate muttered. "Easy enough for them to say, when they have families to go home to. They have no idea what my life is like. I'm forty-seven years old and tired of being a workaholic for the sake of the literary world." *Or to compensate for the lack of a companion,* he mentally added.

He thought of the eligible girls and women he had known, often introduced to him by matchmaking friends. None had impressed him enough to share more than an occasional dinner. Long experience had taught him that they were more interested in N. Alexander—sometimes likened by critics to John Grisham—than in Nate as a man.

During the past several months, Nathan had recognized a growing dissatisfaction with his life and himself. He'd chalked it up to fatigue and identifying so closely with the hero of *The Overcomer.* Now the prospect of continuing on the writing and speaking merry-go-round that had whirled him from deadline to deadline was repugnant. He broke into a long lope, trying to outrun his restlessness. It dogged his steps closer than a shadow and brought him to a monumental decision just as he reached Fisherman's Wharf. Summer was over; autumn and winter lay ahead. Now that *The Overcomer* was finished, he would refuse to give in to his publisher's and editor's pleas for more.

"I need to be among people who demand nothing of me," he decided. "First, I have to make it clear I am *not* going to start another novel until I'm good and ready, whether it's January or June or a year from now." The promise of freedom mingled with the breeze off the bay. It reminded Nate of distant school days, when the school bell heralding the beginning of vacation sounded. He couldn't remember when he had felt so exhilarated. Now all he had to do was to decide where he would go in order to find the companionship he craved.

His answer wasn't long in coming. When he reached his hotel, he discovered an invitation from an old college friend. Their class was having a long-overdue reunion, a weekend house party at the home of a classmate whose wise investments had kept him affluent even in these shaky times. Could Nathan come?

Nate sent his acceptance the same day. He also called his editor and broke the news of his impending sabbatical. The phone line reverberated with protest, but Nate held firm. "I have to get away. Yes, I have ideas for other novels. . . . No, I am *not* going to start one anytime soon. . . . If I don't back off, I'll burn out." He hung up the phone, feeling good about himself. The next few months would counteract the effect of the sacrifices he had made for far too long.

Laughter and good cheer abounded at the house party. It was great to knit together the years between college and the present. However, it didn't lessen Nate's awareness that while he supposedly had it all, there was still an emptiness inside him. Not even old acquaintances and half-forgotten friendships could fill it.

❧

At his former roommate's insistence, Nate signed up for a cruise planned as a follow-up to the house party. To his dismay, however, reminiscences soon began to bore him. He stole away to a quiet spot on the deck as often as he could without being discourteous. He loved the rolling waves that stretched to the distant horizon. They reminded him of Rudyard Kipling's "The Explorer."

Nate's pulse quickened, the same way it had when Mrs. Sorenson, his junior high language arts teacher, first read the poem in class. Although written in 1898, it challenged Nate and set him afire to someday write words that would touch others as deeply as Kipling touched him; to encourage them to listen for God's "everlasting Whisper," and to follow wherever it might lead.

> *"There's no sense in going further—it's the edge of cultivation,"*
> *So they said, and I believed it—broke my land and sowed my crop—*
> *Built my barns and strung my fences in the little border station*

> Tucked away below the foothills where the trails run out
> and stop:
> Till a voice, as bad as Conscience, rang interminable changes
> On one everlasting Whisper day and night repeated—so:
> "Something hidden. Go and find it. Go and look behind
> the Ranges—
> "Something lost behind the Ranges. Lost and waiting for
> you. Go!"

Nate and his classmates had sat spellbound, transported by Mrs. Sorenson's dramatic voice to a faraway country where the explorer's ponies froze to death, where terror and despair threatened to overcome him and drive him into madness. Yet through it all, he heard God's "everlasting Whisper," and refused to turn back. How Nate and the others rejoiced when the explorer found food, water, and a land rich with ore, wood, cattle, and "coal and iron at your doors." Then came the thrilling conclusion.

> God took care to hide that country till He judged His people
> ready,
> Then He chose me for His Whisper, and I've found it, and
> it's yours!
> Yes, your "Never-never country"—yes, your "edge of cultivation"
> And "no sense in going further"—till I crossed the range to see.
> God forgive me! No, I didn't. It's God's present to our nation.
> Anybody might have found it, but—His Whisper came to Me!

Nate considered the magnificent words second only to the Bible in literary value. Now he stood at the rail of the ship, watching the far horizon. For many years he had "looked behind the ranges." He had sought and accomplished much. Why did he feel this sense of loss, of having missed something hidden and waiting? Was the "everlasting Whisper" beckoning him? He had to know. During the rest of the cruise, Nate spent a great deal of time in soul-searching. A trusted friend who had mentored him early in his career came to mind, and Nate had the conviction that he should go to him.

≥

Back on land, Nate tracked down his mentor's Denver address, called, and made an appointment. His heart leaped when the plane neared the city after crossing gigantic mountain ranges. Was this where he would find the missing piece?

The atmosphere of the wood-paneled living room in his friend's home encouraged him. A few insightful questions on the part of Nate's host loosed dammed-up floodwaters. Nate talked without interruption for almost two hours. Then he waited.

At last his friend said, "Nathan, You know God. You love Him and write about Him. You are helping change lives with the talent He has given You. Yet from what you have told me, it seems you may be robbing our Master. How long has it been since you put aside your writing *for* Him in order to spend time *with* Him?"

The truth hit Nate like a Greyhound bus. He bowed his head and stared at the hands that had typed millions of words about God, but seldom stilled longer than a few minutes in prayer. "I don't know."

"Is it possible you have made a god of your writing?" the other inquired.

Silence fell into the room like a cloud descending to earth. A minute passed. Two. Five. Nate stood and shook his mentor's hand. "Thank you."

"Godspeed, boy." The old farewell. The old blessing.

Nate stumbled from his mentor's home filled with determination. He returned to San Francisco and stored everything except the clothing and personal effects he planned to take with him. With a farewell wave, he drove through Nevada and into the mountains of Idaho and Montana, then across the Canadian

border. He traveled under his own name. N. Alexander had
no place in this odyssey into a world far from publicity blitzes
and book-signing tours. He chose modest motels instead of
luxury accommodations and never once switched on his laptop
computer. He felt each mile of his journey moving him closer
to the unknown goal that still eluded him.

In Vancouver, B.C., Nate had noticed a brightly colored
brochure touting the city of Victoria, one of the few places
he'd never visited. He immediately set out for Victoria. Its
old-world charm claimed him from the moment he drove off
the ferry. He explored the length and breadth of Vancouver
Island. Some of the small towns reminded him of Alderdale.
Butchart Gardens kindled a spark with their beauty and his-
tory. Someone's dream had changed an ugly quarry into an
exquisite masterpiece, just as God's dreams transformed ugli-
ness into beauty.

Nate visited Butchart Gardens again and again. The burning desire to write returned. Not another novel, although he
had material enough for several. Nathan watched a tiny
hummingbird probe a nearby honeysuckle blossom for nec-
tar. The sight solidified his longing. "I want to write my life
story," he said, "to dig into the past and find all it has to
offer. It won't be for publication. Just for me, a search for the
boy who began to slip away at my first success." He lapsed
into silence, wishing for simpler days, simpler ways. "Is it
true you can't ever go home again, as Thomas Wolfe says?"
He wished he could. Fame had come at a high cost: Passing
years had touched his dark hair with silver and stolen some
of the laughter from his midnight-black eyes.

The hummingbird moved on, just as Nate had moved on
so many times. He set his jaw. Not this time. He would lease
a place that overlooked the water and was equipped for
housekeeping. There he would begin writing his memoirs.

Nate miraculously found just what he wanted that same

afternoon. The furnished cottage felt like home. The harbor view from the living room was incomparable. Half-forgotten memories pounded at the door of Nate's mind and demanded admittance while he shopped for groceries. He didn't stop to unpack his clothes; he just put away his food and unearthed his laptop. The *click-click* of his fingers on the keyboard resembled the sound of hail on a metal roof.

A clock on a nearby public building chimed twelve before Nate stopped typing. He hit Spell Check, stretched, and laughed. Years before he owned a computer, he'd had his own personal spell-checker: a brown-haired girl promoted to his Advanced Language Arts class in junior high school. *Where was Emily Ann Carr now?* he wondered. He never used Spell Check without remembering her.

"My spelling is no better than it was then," he admitted. "That girl sure was a big help. I never found a copy editor who could spell as well as Em'ly Ann. Her eyes always shone when I read what I considered were masterpieces. Too bad we moved away from Alderdale. I'd have liked getting better acquainted with her."

He stared out the window at the lights blossoming in the harbor. Emily Ann's writing had been unique. It had been difficult for her to read in class. No wonder, the way some of their fellow students treated her. "Probably jealous of her talent," Nate surmised. His thoughts rushed on. Had life given her the opportunity to develop her budding skills? Probably not. He'd never seen her byline anywhere.

Nate sighed. He'd never know. A second thought followed. Even if she read N. Alexander's books, Emily Ann would have no reason to suspect the author was the boy she used to help with his spelling. She wouldn't know the far-reaching effects of her help and encouragement The idea depressed him. He shut off his computer and went to bed.

The next morning, Nathan continued his task. He found

himself savoring his return to childhood. Word pictures of frosty waterfalls and forest glades crept into his story. He'd never before appreciated how deeply Alderdale had influenced his writing. Things had been so different then. Right was right, wrong was wrong, and never the twain should meet. Nate's books always upheld good over evil. Now the reliving of his early years strengthened his early exposure to the simplicity of Jesus' teachings and brought him closer to his heavenly Father.

ða

One day the fan mail forwarded by Nate's publisher included a letter with *Emily Ann Carr* written in the upper left corner of the envelope above an Alderdale, Oregon, address. Nate stared. Why would his long-ago friend write to him after all these years? Perhaps it was a different Emily Ann Carr. If not, the girl he once knew evidently hadn't married. Why not? If she had stayed as sweet and pretty as when she was a girl, any man would be proud and blessed to have her for his wife.

Any man? Nathan nodded. Any man, including him, if he wanted a wife. He grunted. It was uncanny to hear from her when she'd so recently been on his mind. The next moment, his delight over the unopened letter gave way to common sense. The letter was addressed to Mr. N. Alexander.

"What did you expect?" Nate rebuked himself. "No way could Em'ly Ann connect us. It would be nice to see her again. She may be a mother and grandmother and have kept her maiden name." He shook his head and sighed. It was probably better to remember her as she used to be, rather than risk the disillusionment that often comes from renewing old friendships.

The letter was exactly what Nate would have expected. Emily Ann explained her writing assignment and went on to relate how *The Seeker* had inspired her. She focused on several points that Nate felt represented the essence of the book well. She ended by writing:

Whether this book wins awards, as some of your other titles have, isn't nearly as important as the encouragement it offers to those bound by the "everydayness" of life, as well as by major obstacles.

I am sure many readers will be blessed by the example your courageous hero set. Yet if I were the only one, The Seeker *still needed to be written.*

Nate had never felt more humble. Gratitude mingled with the knowledge that Emily Ann's letter had taken him another step nearer to finding what he sought. The wish to learn more about her grew. Why not correspond with her, but as N. Alexander? He would soon learn whether she remained as delightful as the young girl who encouraged him in his dreams. Mischief surged through him. "I'll plant hints to my identity with occasional misspellings and see how long it takes for her to catch on," he decided.

Nate grinned in anticipation, feeling younger than January and more lighthearted than he'd been in years.

five

From the time Emily Carr was big enough to toddle to the mailbox, she considered it one of the most exciting places in her small world. Rain or shine, she seldom missed waiting for the mail carrier. He often teased her and adapted the U.S. Postal Service's motto into, *"Neither snow, nor rain, nor heat, nor gloom of night stays Miss Emily from meeting me at her mailbox."*

"You bring wonderful things," she replied, hugging the day's mail.

He never failed to raise a bushy eyebrow and say, "Mostly advertisements."

Emily always politely nodded, but she could never resist telling him, "They are such *wonderful* advertisements!" Their little joke continued until he retired years later.

Emily's joy of getting the mail never faded. She loved the anticipation that sped through her just before she opened the box. She always hesitated with one hand on the latch, savoring the moment. What lurked inside? A letter from Aunt Carolyn? A Sears & Roebuck or Montgomery Ward "wish book," filled with promise? How many happy hours Emily and Davey had spent making lists and selecting all the things they would have "someday." As an adult, Emily marveled over their joy. Both had always known the treasures described wouldn't be theirs, at least not for a long, long time.

Years passed. The mailbox delivered other treasures. Emily vicariously lived Davey's experiences at church camp, financed by a newspaper route that roused him from sleep before dawn. If a tear dropped to the boyish scribbling, she made certain no one ever saw it except God. Emily would erase all signs of wishing she could be enjoying camp with her brother before reading the letter to their father.

Changes came for Davey. They did not come for Emily. School and being the woman of the family took time and hard work. After Davey went to college, letters signed "David" marked the passing of boy into man. Marriage, the birth of Bill and Danielle, and the departure of David's wife followed. Because of David's military career, Emily became both mother and father to the children. Life continued, with the mailbox containing "Dear Aunt Emily" letters from a second generation of church camps.

When David was sent to the Middle East, Emily had a hard time getting to the mailbox before young Bill and Danielle. Overseas letters were infrequent. The three "home-front soldiers," as David called them, read the few letters that did come, until they were ragged.

One day a letter addressed only to Emily arrived. It amply rewarded her for the long stay-at-home years and gave her the courage to continue her task. David wrote:

> *You will never know what it has meant to me to know you are carrying on, while I am half a world away trying to prevent individuals who lust for power from destroying America and the world. The knowledge that my children are being trained as we were gives me peace of mind. Thank you.*
>
> *Emily Ann, if I'm not permitted to return to Alderdale, take heart. We will meet again. I am more confident of this than ever. I've felt the Spirit of God working in my life, and have taken Romans 8:38–39 for my watchword. "For I am convinced that neither death nor life, neither angels nor demons, neither the present nor the future, nor any powers, neither height nor depth, nor anything else in all creation, will be able to separate us from the love of God, that is in Christ Jesus our Lord." Now I add, nor from each other.*

For the first time in years the letter was signed: *"Your Davey."*

Emily folded the pages and slowly returned them to their envelope. That evening, she read the latter half of the letter to Bill and Danielle, carefully omitting her brother's special message to her. Danielle scooted closer to Emily. Bill said, "I'm glad Dad wrote like that, just in case. . ." He strode from the room, chin up, shoulders squared, a replica of his courageous pilot father.

That was David's last letter.

৯

With Bill married and relocated to Arizona, his letters helped fill the mailbox and Emily's empty heart. So did Danielle's. Hers were filled with a jumble of excitement, homesickness, and reflections on how different Boston and the university she was attending were from Alderdale. When she learned Emily had signed up for a writing course, she sent a letter via Federal Express that contained only two words: "Go, girl!" Emily grinned, but she appreciated her niece's approval and support.

The more practical Bill responded by phone. "You've never wanted a computer, but you need one if you're going to be a world-famous author. Now that you can afford it, get yourself good equipment and take a computer class. Get rid of the old typewriter Danielle and I left there. I know a guy who'll give you a good deal on a computer, and he'd be happy to get you set up."

"Computer? World-famous author?" Emily laughed into the phone. "You must be joking."

"No way. You'll have Internet access for market and other research, plus e-mail, which means we can keep in touch with Danielle and each other more frequently. It's cheaper than phone calls and easier than writing letters. C'mon, Aunt Emily, be a sport."

She signed up for a computer class at a nearby community center the following day. Emily also gave Bill a go-ahead to contact his friend. By the end of the week they had converted a small, unused room that overlooked her tree-filled backyard, into an office. She began her new class, heartened by her nephew's phone calls. His "You can do it!" spurred her on. So did the patient teacher who never made her students feel stupid when they asked questions.

Even Emily's exciting classes couldn't overcome the disappointment about her unanswered letter to N. Alexander. Her instructor read it aloud in class, considerately omitting her name. Emily's classmates' comments were as positive as the large red "A" it earned for clarity, brevity, and sincerity. It gave her courage to polish a long-dormant children's story, take a deep breath, and read it in class. The story earned praise and excellent suggestions for improvement from both the instructor and fellow students.

Emily hadn't really expected a personal reply from her favorite author, but anyone so famous as N. Alexander surely had a secretary to answer fan mail. It seemed strange that she hadn't received so much as a printed acknowledgment.

Late one afternoon, Emily fled home for refuge after another unavoidable and especially unpleasant encounter with Herman Dobbs. The stolid man had persisted in walking down Main Street with her, then waiting for her outside the library. Emily shuddered to think how Alderdale would jump to conclusions. She told Herman pointblank, "I don't care to walk with you. Good-bye."

It did no good. He simply smirked and said, "I can bide my time." It took all of Emily's Christian charity to keep from telling him to go chase himself.

For once, even checking the mail held no appeal. She jerked open her mailbox. Empty. Either the carrier was late or she had received no mail. Emily walked into the house and burst out to Sister Feline, "I'm beginning to feel like a prisoner in my own town! There must be a Dobbs child spying on me from behind every tree. Otherwise, how would that father of theirs know every time I leave the house?"

She took Sister Feline's plaintive "meow" for agreement and rushed on. "One of these days. . ." The sound of the mail truck cut off her dire threat. Instead of rushing outside, she watched from the window. The carrier was putting an envelope in her box. Good. A letter from Bill or Danielle would do wonders in taking her mind off Herman Dobbs. She hurried outside and opened her mailbox.

The envelope lay address-side down. Long, white, and fat, it little resembled the envelopes Bill and Danielle sent. Emily turned it over and peered at the return address. Her spirits shot from the depths to the heights. It was from the publisher that presented N. Alexander's books to his salivating public!

"They must have stuffed it with brochures of upcoming titles," Emily reflected. Too keyed up to wait until she was back inside, she ripped off the stamped end and gasped. There were no brochures. Just several closely typed pages.

"I see you have an official-looking letter, Miss Carr." Herman Dobbs's grating voice jarred Emily from her absorption. "If it's about your inheritance, I'd be glad to help. I have a lot of experience with legal issues."

Resenting being interrupted and cheated of her initial pleasure in the letter, she glared into the man's snooping face. "My correspondence is none of your concern whatsoever," she told him. "Furthermore, if I see you near my mailbox again, I will report you to the U.S. Postal Service for interference."

The man's mouth dropped open. "I-I wasn't. . ."

"Well, see that you don't," Emily snapped. She turned and forced herself to walk up the path to her porch without looking back. The dull tread of Herman's clodhopper boots on the gravel outside her fence proclaimed his more-than-welcome departure.

Good heavens, where did that come from? she wondered.

There was no law preventing Herman Dobbs from standing near her mailbox.

Emily's jangled nerves were not conducive to enjoying her much-anticipated letter. She forced herself to drink a cup of tea and make a casserole for supper before settling down on the couch with Sister Feline curled up close beside her.

> *Dear Miss Carr,*
>   *I apologize for not having answered your letter sooner. I have been traveling, and it only caught up with me today—in beautiful Victoria on Vancouvre Island. You'll never know how glad I am that you signed up for the writing class and chose me for your first assignment. I've been going through a frustrating time in my life and career. I needed to hear exactly what you had to say.*

Astonished, Emily reread the words. This was no routine acknowledgment, but a highly personal letter from the author! Her fingers shook, and she read on.

> *For some time I have sensed a growing discontent with my life, a feeling of something missing. I pushed it aside until I met the deadline for* The Overcomer, *which you'll be pleased to learn is a sequel to* The Seeker. *I believe it is the best work I have done.*

Emily paused again. How wonderful to have such a book to look forward to reading! She eagerly returned to the letter. N. Alexander shared how his old mentor helped him realize he had allowed his writing to overshadow his personal relationship with his heavenly Father. He told how his sojourn to "Vancouvre" Island and Butchart Gardens gave him a whole new closeness with God.

Emily smiled at the spelling of Vancouver. Evidently, Mr. Alexander hadn't used Spell Check. Memories of Nathan

Hamilton returned. His face was as clear in her mind as it had been more than thirty years ago. How they'd shared the joy of being praised by Mrs. Sorenson when one of them wrote a story that pleased her!

There was more, much more, before N. Alexander ended his letter.

> *Is this your first writing class? How is it going? Have you been interested in writing for a long time, or is it a new pursuit? If all your work is as interesting and well-written as your letter, you certainly should pursue the writing craft. I hope you will write to me again at my Victoria address below. I can't begin to express how your comments lifted me up at a time I most needed to hear exactly what you wrote.*

Never in her wildest imagination had Emily dreamed she would receive such a personal letter from an author, especially one she deeply admired. It left her overwhelmed with gratitude. It wasn't so much that Mr. Alexander had taken the time to write. What touched her most were the words: "If all your work is as interesting and well-written as your letter, you certainly should pursue the writing craft." They danced through her mind, bringing confirmation that the faltering steps she had taken were in the right direction.

That night Emily prayed long and earnestly about her future. She finished by saying, "Lord, this day has been a roller-coaster ride. From Herman Dobbs to N. Alexander— what a leap! It seems it would be rude not to answer Mr. Alexander's letter. He must be sincere about wanting me to respond or he wouldn't have asked all those questions."

She fell asleep in the middle of her "amen." She awoke clear-headed. She would wait a week before she responded to Mr. Alexander's letter. That way, there was no danger she would appear forward.

ื

Emily received an answer to her second letter—it was filled with more questions—by return mail. Then she received another. And another. She realized she was beginning to look forward to the renowned author's letters far too much and laid down the law. "Emily Ann Carr, stop acting like a schoolgirl with her first crush," she chastised. "Stop this racing to the mailbox, your heart pounding like a sprinter after a hundred-yard dash. Have your manless years, broken only by wannabe suitors the caliber of Herman Dobbs, made you desperate? The only thing that can come from this is heartache. N. Alexander will tire of corresponding and go back to the world in which he belongs. A world in which you can never be a part."

Emily's scolding was to no avail. She rebelliously wrote in her journal:

> *So what if it happens that way? He will never know how I feel, and I may never again have anything so wonderful happen to me. Mr. Alexander has never hinted at anything more than sharing his thoughts and feelings in our letters, but he's given me a touch of the romance I've longed for. One day he will go away, just as Nathan Hamilton did—but I will still have my memories.*

Her burst of independence should have settled the question. It didn't. In desperation, she called Aunt Carolyn and asked her advice, carefully omitting her own growing feelings. "Should I continue writing to Mr. Alexander?"

"Go ahead. Anyone who writes the way he does isn't likely to wind up on the Most Wanted list," was her forthright aunt's half-serious reply.

Emily hung up, laughed until tears came, and began writing another letter.

six

Nate Alexander riffled through his just-delivered letters and impatiently tossed them aside. For the past ten days he'd eagerly awaited the mail, only to be as bitterly disappointed as a child who reaches into a cookie jar and finds it empty. There had been plenty of time for Emily Ann Carr to answer his letter, even considering possible delays due to his being in Victoria.

"Seems like she could at least answer," he grumped. "The Em'ly Ann I knew would have." Unwilling to stay inside with only his disgruntled self for company, Nate caught up a warm jacket and the keys to his car. At least the weather was cooperating. Fall had fallen. Literally. Golden maple leaves and the red of sumac punctuated the landscape. Another visit to Butchart Gardens would help restore his spirits. In spite of an early morning frost that had increased the color spectrum of the leaves, hardy roses and a multitude of perennials continued to bloom.

The western sun was flinging a lingering good night to the island when Nate drove away from his temporary home. In all his travels, he had seldom seen sunsets comparable to those in Victoria. No artist or photographer could ever capture the panorama of red, gold, orange, and cerise, spreading over the water to mantle the land with a rosy glow. The first star broadcast a light signal for hosts of its comrades to appear. A full moon crept up over the horizon and promised a spectacular drive.

"I wish. . ." Nate sighed. Even though his time in Victoria had brought the presence of the Master more deeply into his life, how wonderful it would be to have a companion, especially at times like this. A world that caught at one's throat with its beauty was meant to be shared. No wonder God had said in Genesis, "It is not good for man to be alone. I will make a helper suitable for him."

Nate had never felt the need of a helper enough to consider praying about it.

Until now.

Ever since that fateful morning in San Francisco, the feeling that he stood on the precipice of change had lurked in the back of Nate's mind. His old mentor's counsel had turned his thoughts toward God. So far, his odyssey had proved satisfying, although he recognized he still had far to go to find the "something lost and hidden" waiting behind the ranges of his future.

Will part of it be love and marriage? he wondered, while purple dusk crouched on the horizon before fleeing from the approaching night. He uneasily shifted position in his seat. After years of flying solo, could he change his thinking from "me" to "we" and be a good husband?

Nate laughed in derision at the thought of what kind of husband he would make, with no prospects of a wife in sight. "Hmm. I wonder what Em'ly Ann would think of such a preposterous idea?"

As if you'd tell her, his conscience jeered.

Laughter died as suddenly as it had been born. "It looks like I'll never have the chance to tell her that or anything else," Nate said. A pang went through him. He wouldn't have believed how much contentment could come from sharing his struggles, as he had done in the letter that hadn't been answered. He would never have risked writing it if he hadn't known her years ago.

"The problem is, Em'ly Ann doesn't have a clue I'm anyone except an author she admires. Having a total stranger write the way I did may have offended her."

Nate mulled it over until he reached Butchart Gardens. The lights of San Francisco reflecting in the bay were no more impressive than the scene that lay before him. Artificial lighting paled by comparison to the fully risen moon. A slight breeze harvested perfume from hundreds of drowsy roses.

Nate sauntered through the gardens, then climbed to a high point where he could be alone with the night. He listened to the song of fountains and waterfalls until his hands and face chilled and the desire for companionship drove him back among strangers—strangers who would offer occasional smiles and greetings. As N. Alexander, he'd grown tired of the multitude that surrounded and drained him with their demands. Like other authors who shot from obscurity to fame after long years of slow but steady growth, he'd been besieged by those asking him to speak, teach, and mentor.

"I spent a lot of time and energy learning I couldn't be all things to all people," Nate said quietly, his voice tinged with regret. "It's nice to be incognito for a time. Mr. A. Nonymous in person."

Nice, but lonely. Right?

"Right." Held captive by the night and his ambivalence, Nate drove home and headed for his computer. Writing normally freed him from daily irritations. It also often brought answers to his most perplexing questions when the characters he created faced similar situations. Now he decided, "If I can't find what I need in the present, I'll look for it in the past."

Hours later, Nate yawned, switched off the computer, and went to bed. His journey into yesterday had succeeded in replacing his gloom with hope. A new day lay waiting just beyond the horizon. Would it bring a letter from Alderdale?

❧

Nate was not disappointed the next day. He read the new letter twice: the first time for content, the second for enjoyment. He marveled at Emily Ann's ability to paint with words. Her description of Alderdale made him long to drop everything and rush back to the small-town way of life he'd almost forgotten still existed.

He shook his head. "No. It's too soon. One good thing, though: Em'ly Ann sure sounds like the girl I knew in junior high. The value of her writing is in its simplicity. She must remember Mrs. Sorenson telling the class, especially me, 'Less is more. Don't attack readers with bursts of adjectives and adverbs.' Em'ly Ann always could make one word say what she wanted."

Nate chuckled. "I can't go home yet, but I can keep writing letters loaded with questions. It will keep Em'ly Ann corresponding, even if only to be polite!"

&

During the rest of the fall and early winter, letters flew like carrier pigeons between Oregon and Victoria, B.C. With every letter, Emily continued to fight a losing battle with her unruly heart. All the telling herself she was behaving foolishly didn't stop her traitorous heart from hammering or prevent warm color from rushing to her face when she read her messages. She wrote in her journal:

> *What I am feeling is probably hero worship, nothing more. Gaggles of silly women fall in love with well-known authors. I've always despised their foolishness. Now I'm dangerously close to joining their ranks!*
>
> *All I know about romance is what I've read in books and through daydreams about a boy who has long since forgotten me. I should be ashamed of myself for trying to find more in Mr. Alexander's letters than what is there.*

Isn't there more? Unsophisticated as she was in matters of the heart, the growing affection in N. Alexander's letters seemed obvious. Emily continued writing.

He evidently sees worth in my writing and is kind enough
to encourage me. He's never asked how old I am. That shows
he has no interest in me except as a correspondent while he is
far away from his friends.

She snapped the journal shut and scooped up Sister Feline
from a nearby chair. "Enough acting like a moonstruck schoolgirl," she firmly told her cat, feeling she had won this skir-
mish—but aware the war between common sense and
long-suppressed hopes raged on, fueled by every letter from
Victoria, misspellings and all.

A few days later, the sharp ring of Emily's doorbell interrupted her inadequate attempts to send an e-mail attachment
to Bill. She made a face and didn't answer.

The ringing persisted, followed by a voice calling, "Miss
Emily? Are you home?"

Emily glanced out the window. The local florist's delivery
van was parked by her gate. She gave thanks that it wasn't
Elmer Dobbs or Harriet Taylor and hurried to the door, Sister
Feline at her heels. "Sorry. I've been trying to conquer e-mail."

"Good for you." The florist, who had served the town's
needs for decades, held an enormous arrangement of roses,
carnations, and decorative ferns. A handful of blue forget-
me-nots nestled in the center.

Emily gasped. "My goodness! That's not a bouquet; it's an
entire garden!"

"Would you like me to carry this inside? The crystal vase is
pretty heavy."

"Please put it on the hall table, if you would." She held the
screen door open.

"Sure. There's no card. It was ordered anonymously." He
set the flowers down. "Someone sure admires you, Miss
Emily. But then, everyone does," the florist added. "Good
luck tracking down the sender." He touched his forehead in

an old-fashioned salute of respect and whistled his way back to the delivery van.

No card? Someone admires me? Indignation flooded through Emily. "Is this another attempt by Herman Dobbs to ingratiate himself?" she demanded of Sister Feline. Doubt crept in. Surely the rude man wouldn't spend so much money on his wife-finding campaign—not even to obtain a mother for his children.

Oh, yeah? a warning voice mocked. *The cost of the flowers is a pittance compared with the vast fortune he and Harriet think you inherited. If Herman Dobbs sent the flowers, he will consider it an investment in his future.*

The thought was so repulsive, Emily reached for the bouquet, fully intending to throw it into the street. When her unwelcome suitor passed by, he'd see what she thought of his tactics. Common sense prevailed. "He may not have sent it," Emily told her cat. "I can't imagine Herman Dobbs, or even Harriet Taylor, being subtle enough to include the forget-me-nots. Neither seems the anonymous-acts-of-kindness type. Even if they were, it's been years since anyone sent me flowers. My last were from Aunt Carolyn, when I graduated from high school. Why deprive myself of the pleasure they will bring?" She buried her nose in the fragrant bouquet. "Besides, they aren't Herman Dobbs's flowers. They were originally God's. Now they're mine." Sister Feline rubbed against Emily's ankles and began to purr.

❧

A week later, Emily Ann found a package in her mailbox. The return address was a specialty bookstore in Portland. Strange. She'd never ordered anything from them. It must be a mistake. On the other hand, it could be one of those promotional advertisements, where companies send out books in hopes of gaining customers by hooking them with the first title of a new series.

This was not the case. Safe in her living room, hidden from possible prying eyes, Emily opened her package. To her amazement, it was a beautiful, leather-bound edition of *Little Women*. The name *Emily Ann Carr* was engraved in gold on the cover.

She couldn't believe it. Who would send her such a gift, and for no apparent reason? Christmas was weeks away; her birthday long since past. This couldn't be Herman Dobbs's doing. Even if he were to send a book, he had no way of knowing *Little Women* was one of Emily's all-time favorites. Neither did Harriet.

Emily felt a blush start at the neckline of her modest blue house dress and creep upward. Was it possible that. . . ? She shook her head. "If Mr. Alexander were kind enough to send me a book, it would be one of his titles that we discussed. We've never talked about Louisa May Alcott's work and how much I like her writing." She ran her fingers over the golden letters of her name and told her omnipresent cat, "Now we have two mysteries. I never did find out who sent the flowers, just who didn't. If Herman Dobbs were responsible, he'd try to move heaven and earth to make sure I and everyone else in Alderdale knew it!"

Sister Feline cocked her head to one side and looked wise.

❧

Encouraged by N. Alexander's praise for her interesting letters, Emily Ann dug out a few children's stories she'd made up for her brother and, later, for his children. Their quality surprised her. Even those written when she was quite young had a certain charm and appeal. She diligently polished them, using all the skills her eager mind was absorbing in her writing class.

"You may wish to try submitting them," her instructor told her.

Emily shook her head. "I'm not that confident yet." She didn't explain she wouldn't get to that stage until Mr. Alexander had seen a story. She definitely wasn't ready for *that*, even though he'd invited her to send samples of her writing.

Emily Ann continued to spend a great deal of time in prayer concerning her deepening attraction for her "by mail" friend. At last she "dumped it all in God's lap," as she told Sister Feline, and was rewarded with the peace she badly needed.

2a

Three hundred miles north of Alderdale, autumn flew south with the wild geese. Stark, leafless branches warned that winter lingered just around the corner. The feeling he needed to return to Oregon before he could finish his memoirs haunted Nathan Hamilton day and night. So did the knowledge that letters were a poor substitute for love.

The advantage of knowing with whom he was corresponding had served him well. On paper, Emily Ann was the same girl he'd known long ago, only more mature.

One wild afternoon, when rain pelted Nate's cottage, he knelt beside his bed and surrendered himself to his growing feelings. "Thank You for leading me here, God," he prayed. "I've found what I was missing for so long: a more personal relationship with You. I also feel Em'ly Ann may be the companion I need and Your answer to my loneliness. Am I the right husband for her? N. Alexander already has her friendship and admiration. Will it grow into love for plain old Nate Hamilton?"

There was only one way to find out. Just before Christmas, Nate wrote a letter designed to play on Emily Ann Carr's sympathies and put him back into her life.

seven

Early one nippy autumn morning, Emily received a call from Isaiah Gerard.

"I need to see you," he said brusquely. "As soon as you can get here."

The lawyer sounded so unlike himself, an alarm bell went off in Emily's mind. "Right away. Does this have anything to do with my inheritance?"

"It has everything to do with your inheritance," Isaiah snapped. "I'll tell you more when I see you." He broke the connection.

Emily stared at the silent phone and slowly replaced it in its cradle. Never before had her friend spoken to her in such a manner. There must be something terribly wrong or the usually unflappable Isaiah Gerard wouldn't have hung up without the courtesy of a good-bye! With a quick prayer for strength, Emily hurried to change from nightgown and robe into warm clothing. She hastily donned her navy suit and arranged the scarlet scarf with nervous fingers.

Her shadow, Sister Feline, extended a paw toward Emily's pantyhose and meowed indignantly when her owner pushed her away. Emily barely heard her. She rushed downstairs and out the door, leaving her cat complaining in the hall.

Main Street lay mercifully empty, except for a few parked vehicles with heavily frosted tops and windshields. Emily Ann traversed its length in record time. Her cheeks burned with cold when she reached the law offices of Gerard & Son.

Isaiah's warm welcome contrasted sharply with the way he had sounded on the phone. *Surely there couldn't be* too *much wrong,* Emily thought.

"Sit down, sit down," the white-haired attorney boomed. "Hmm. You are certainly looking well. You must have walked. Your cheeks are brighter than your scarf." His eyes twinkled. "You should wear red more often, Em'ly Ann. It makes you look young."

Emily felt a flutter of pleasure at his compliment. "Thank you. I feel young. It's all I can do to keep from skipping up and down the streets."

Isaiah threw his head back and laughed heartily. "That I'd like to see." An instant later, a frown appeared and spread. He picked up a pen from his desk and dropped a bombshell. "What's this I hear about you getting married?"

Emily felt hot color surge into her face. Mr. Gerard *couldn't* know she'd thought a lot about marriage lately. She had never confessed her growing desire for a companion except in prayer and to Sister Feline. "Wh–who told you that?"

Isaiah's face set in an expression of stern disapproval. "So it's true? Em'ly Ann Carr, I'm disappointed in you. You are far too good for Herman Dobbs. Furthermore—"

"Herman Dobbs!" It came out as a strangled whisper.

"Yes, Herman Dobbs. I worked late last night, and he slouched in here trying to get information concerning the size of your inheritance." Isaiah mimicked his visitor to a tone. " 'As Emily Carr's intended, I have the right to know how things stand.' " Isaiah scowled and bent his pen so hard, it snapped in two.

Emily tried to collect her scattered wits. She couldn't believe even Herman Dobbs would go so far! "What did you tell him?" she faltered.

Isaiah scowled. "I asked him to leave. He muttered and sputtered and threatened to have my license revoked; for what, I don't know. About that time my son walked in. He threw Herman out. You aren't *really* going to marry that lout, are you, Em'ly Ann?"

"Marry him! I can't get rid of him!" She sat bolt upright in her chair. "Herman Dobbs, ably abetted by Harriet Taylor, is making my life a nightmare. He squeezes past people at church so he can sit next to me. He insists on walking with me when I go downtown. Lately, he's been strolling past my place and waving at the house. Anyone who sees him is sure to think I'm returning his greetings." Tears of frustration crowded behind her eyelids. Emily held her eyes open wide to keep them from falling.

Her attorney grunted. "It figures." He paused, then leaned forward with his usual kindly look. "Too bad there's no law against extreme annoyance." Isaiah shrugged his shoulders expressively. "Of course, persuasion is my business. Tell you what, I'll call Dobbs in and give him something to think about." A gleam of mischief danced in the attorney's eyes. "I can be quite firm on occasion."

The blatant understatement tickled Emily's funny bone. Isaiah Gerard's cross-examination of lying witnesses was legendary in the state of Oregon. Emily grinned. He could be quite firm, all right! A half-hour later, she left the office feeling freer than she'd been since Harriet Taylor imported her obnoxious cousin-in-law. Her euphoria didn't last long, though; Harriet lay in wait.

"I am. . .so glad. . .I caught you!" Harriet panted between words. She had obviously spotted her prey while Emily talked with Isaiah on the steps of the law office and had run to catch up with her. "Is there anything new concerning your inheritance?"

Emily limited her reply to, "Good morning, Harriet. It's another nice day."

"Not so nice for some," the other woman said. "Dear Herman is heartbroken and distraught at the way you are treating him. How can a good Christian woman like you refuse to take pity on him and his children in their hour of need?"

Hour of need? Harriet sounded like a low-budget soap-opera character.

Emily stifled her mirth. "I'm sorry, Harriet. I've said everything I care to say on the subject of Mr. Dobbs.

"Tell me, though," Emily continued. "How are things going for the community Thanksgiving dinner? You're in charge this year, aren't you?"

The ploy to sidetrack her adversary worked. Harriet bridled with pleasure. "Yes. It's going to be the best dinner ever." She launched into a detailed, glowing description of decorations, menu, and planned entertainment.

For the first time, Emily saw past Harriet's meddling to the woman's deep-seated need to be appreciated by more than her daughter Amelia. If Harriet had been blessed with grandchildren, perhaps it wouldn't have been necessary for her to seek attention by interfering in the lives of others. Pity temporarily erased Emily's annoyance and softened her voice. "It sounds wonderful. What would you like me to bring?"

"Pumpkin pies. Three, if you will. You make the best pies in Alderdale."

Emily felt her lips twitch. No one could turn a compliment into a flat statement of fact like Harriet Taylor. A few minutes later they parted, with no further discussion of Herman Dobbs's state of mind and heart.

When Emily arrived home, she checked her mailbox and gave it a surreptitious pat. It continued to provide moments of delicious anticipation, but so had her entry into the world of e-mail. Once she'd mastered its intricacies, it offered the same feeling of being on the brink of wonderful things that her faithful mailbox had provided since childhood. Emily held her breath each time she hit Get New Mail, wondering how many messages waited for her. She hadn't yet confessed to N. Alexander that she had e-mail.

Messages displayed on a screen might not seem as exciting as those that came in fat white envelopes.

"How much I've changed in the past few months," Emily murmured. "Even Mr. Gerard said so." The same thrill she'd felt in his office inched through her. "So he thinks red makes me look young and that I should wear it more often. Maybe I will."

The desire for another shopping trip seized her. Most of her earlier purchases were more suitable to summer and fall than the cold season lurking just out of sight. Winter had already laid a gentle hand on the higher hills, leaving a frosting of white that foreshadowed more to come. Snow shovels were prominently displayed amidst the Thanksgiving and Christmas decorations in some of the stores on Main Street.

For the rejuvenated Emily Carr, to think was to act. The following morning found her back at the mall in Portland, reveling in the variety of warm clothing available. She selected skirts and slacks, then chose pretty sweaters to mix and match with their darker colors. A turquoise skirt and twin sweater set joined the pile to be purchased. So did a fisherman's knit sweater, something she'd always longed to own.

Emily turned toward the cashier, experiencing a moment of déjà vu. Except this time, the mannequin wore a holly berry red dress instead of a navy blue suit and scarlet scarf.

I want that dress.

Had she spoken aloud? Emily glanced both ways. No one was paying any attention to her. The dour faces of ultra-conservative ancestors came to mind. Their forbidding expressions clearly indicated what *they* thought of such apparel.

Was she going to let long-dead ancestors dictate to her? No. Emily steadied her voice and said, "I'd like to try on the red dress, please."

"It will look lovely with your brown-and-silver hair," the saleswoman told her.

Emily dismissed the comment as part of the woman's sales technique, until she put on the dress. Its soft folds fell about her as if it had been expertly fashioned for her by a couture. *What would Mr. Alexander think if he saw me now?* Emily wondered. The blush that sprang to her mirrored reflection rivaled the dress in color and tipped the scales. Even though there was little chance she would ever meet N. Alexander, Emily left the store with a jaunty step—and the dress. She'd leave it in her closet until Christmas. It would give her more time to get used to the idea of wearing it. Her newly purchased turquoise skirt and sweater set would do nicely for Thanksgiving.

The bus ride back to Alderdale gave Emily time to reflect on the pleasure she'd felt at the thought of N. Alexander seeing her wearing the exquisite dress. It also reminded her of the silken threads binding her closer to the author with every letter. Doubt crept in. Even though she'd turned her feelings over to God, shouldn't she be making an attempt to regain control over her usual, composed self?

A startling idea came. Perhaps instead of writing off the possibility of a meeting with her correspondent, she should initiate one. It wouldn't be hard. Aunt Carolyn had suggested several times, "If you ever want to meet your boyfriend in person, but don't feel comfortable asking him to visit you in Alderdale, come stay with me. We'll invite him here where you'll both be on neutral ground."

"Thanks, but he isn't my boyfriend, and even if he were, I don't have that much courage," Emily always responded.

Aunt Carolyn invariably sounded skeptical. "Why not? He's been interested enough in you to correspond, hasn't he? If you want something, go for it. Just give me fair warning if you decide to come."

Now her aunt's advice pounded in Emily's brain. It hammered at her all during the successful Thanksgiving dinner, even though Herman Dobbs's baleful gaze reproached her from across the tastefully decorated church fellowship hall, and his five children glowered. Emily Ann didn't know what Mr. Gerard had said to Herman, but it had been enough to make him back off. For how long, Emily didn't know. His biding-my-time expression made her shudder, and the realization that Alderdale still considered her far wealthier than she'd ever be, boded no good for her while Herman Dobbs hung around.

≈

Shortly before Christmas, a pathetic-sounding letter arrived from Canada. N. Alexander praised Emily for her description of the Thanksgiving dinner and those who attended; she had pointedly excluded all mention of Herman Dobbs and his brood! Then he said:

> My mouth watered when you described the turkey, stuffing, pumpkin pies, and all the rest. It reminded me of the "olden days," when parents and grandparents, nieces, nephews, and always a few strays gathered around a table groaning with the weight of good food. Things have certainly changed.
>
> Canada celebrates Thanksgiving in October instead of November. The restaurant where I ate dinner wasn't bad, but it was a far cry from home cooking.
>
> You mentioned your niece and nephew won't be home for Christmas. Do you have any special plans?
>
> I'm great with a microwave and can opener, but not much of a regular cook. I haven't made friends here, only acquaintances. I don't want to impose on them, so I suppose I'll look for a place that will serve a reasonable facsimile of a Christmas dinner. I can't say I look forward to it. Celebrating the birth of Christ all by myself isn't my idea of the way things should be.

Emily didn't know how to respond. She called Aunt Carolyn immediately and read the letter over the phone.

Carolyn snorted. "I've heard some pretty broad hints in my time, but this beats them all. Give me his address. I'll invite him to come to Seattle for the holidays and have Christmas dinner with us."

A few days later, Emily received an e-mail from her aunt. It was crisp, blunt, and exactly like Carolyn. "The glue on my envelope barely had time to dry before your friend's acceptance arrived!"

⋗

When Nathan Hamilton first came up with the idea of appealing to Emily Ann Carr with a "far-from-home-and-family" plea, he also firmly decided to return to Alderdale, regardless of the outcome of the meeting he felt sure would take place. The thrill of "going home" made him feel more like a boy than ever. Love was not just for the young but for those of any age who believed in it and sought it. By the time Carolyn Sheffield's invitation arrived, Nate was "chomping at the bit and raring to go," to use the vernacular of a western story he wrote when he was in junior high. Mrs. Sorenson had torn it up, saying it wasn't worthy of his talent. It wasn't. Even Emily Ann had struggled to keep from laughing when he read it in class.

Packed and ready, Nate faced an obstacle that loomed larger with every passing hour. He paced the floor and considered his problem. "Shall I write and confess who I really am, or wait until I meet Em'ly Ann in Seattle? If I tell her ahead of time, she may not come. If I wait, she will know I finagled the Christmas invitation under false pretenses. Can I convince her that what started as a joke has brought me great happiness? She's never given any indication of picking up on the clues I planted. How will she feel when she learns I've been deceiving her?"

During his long sabbatical, Nate had well learned the

importance of turning to God in everything, not just before making major decisions, although this could certainly be considered one. After a great deal of prayer, he muttered, "The old cliché 'Desperate times call for desperate measures' is right on target." Grinning broadly, he ignored his laptop and picked up pen and paper.

❧

Nathan's letter arrived at the Carr home while Emily was packing. She had just lovingly wrapped her new red dress in tissue paper when the mail arrived. She stared at the hand-written envelope, remembering the day she finally accepted as fact that she truly loved her by-mail friend. Her passionate desire to ensure that Mr. Alexander would never again face another lonely holiday had prevailed, shouting down all her objections. Still she doubted. Was meeting N. Alexander God's will or her own scheme? Even if he one day returned her love, what place could a nobody like Emily Ann Carr have in his world?

Emily walked into the house and tore open the envelope with shaking fingers. A picture and letter fell out. The letter was short and to the point.

> *Dear Emily Ann,*
> *You are in for a surprise. I hope it makes you happy. It does me.*
>
> *N. Alexander*

Emily reread the cryptic message. "How odd. He never calls me Emily Ann." She picked up the picture and stared. A laughing woman stared back from her position between two smiling men. Although the snapshot had evidently been taken from a distance, the beauty of the woman's face could not be denied. Nor could the fact that both men's arms lay across her shoulders. Or the look of joy in all three faces.

Emily turned the snapshot over, hoping to discover which man was her correspondent. There was no identification. "What does this picture have to do with Mr. Alexander's surprise?" she asked Sister Feline.

The cat gave her an unblinking stare.

Emily examined the photograph again. She racked her brain for a logical answer. It came with sickening force, sharp as a heavy stone launched by a strong hand: Mr. Alexander must be bringing a fiancée. He had never mentioned a woman in his letters, but it was difficult to believe there were none in his life. Perhaps someone dear to him was part of the reason he had fled to Victoria. Perhaps they had quarreled and finally resolved their differences. Perhaps. . .

"So what did you expect?" Emily told herself. "That he would fall in love with you? He, a celebrated author? You, a woman beginning the autumn of her life?"

Yes, her heart responded. *That's exactly what I hoped would happen.*

Panicky and on the verge of calling Aunt Carolyn to cancel her visit, Emily turned to her well-read Bible. It fell open to Proverbs 3, and her gaze dropped to verse 6, which she had previously highlighted: "In all thy ways acknowledge him, and he shall direct thy paths."

She laid the Bible aside. For better or worse—and if what she suspected came to pass, it would definitely be worse— she had to go. N. Alexander must never know how much she cherished his friendship. Or to what extent she had hoped it would someday turn to mutual love.

eight

On Christmas Eve morning, Emily Carr clasped her hands in the lap of her navy blue suit and stared out the window of the jetliner, still parked on the Portland tarmac, and thought about the short flight to Seattle. Her heart felt so heavy, she wondered how the plane could lift off and stay in the air long enough to reach their destination. The only bright spots in her world were the brilliant sunshine and the fact that misery over the upcoming ordeal superseded her fear of flying for the first time.

The plane swooshed down the runway and lifted off. The hum of excited conversation and eager faces of those homeward bound surrounded Emily. They made her feel worse than ever. She turned away from them and focused on the retreating landscape below.

I wish I were home. Christmas with only my cat for company would be better than this. Better for her, too.

Emily felt the start of a smile. Spoiled because her mistress was never away from home overnight, Sister Feline had gone into her carrier docilely enough, but threw a cat fit when delivered to the Gerard home. Her black-and-white fur puffed in outrage until she looked twice her normal size. Emily fervently hoped Isaiah and his wife wouldn't regret their cat-sitting offer!

"We'll be arriving at SeaTac International airport shortly," the pilot announced. "Please stay in your seats and fasten your seat belts. We hope you have a pleasant trip."

Emily Ann obeyed his directions and braced herself. Would Mr. Alexander's fiancée be as lovely in person as she was in the hazy photograph? Would she be at the airport? The plane circled and began its descent. Emily riveted her gaze on the earth rushing up to meet her. A psalm that often comforted her when she felt she couldn't go on, came to mind. *"The LORD is my strength and my shield. . . ."* She squared her shoulders, lifted her chin, and prepared to meet one of the hardest trials of her life.

❧

Nate Hamilton arrived in Seattle the morning of December 23. He immediately contacted Ms. Carolyn Sheffield. "If you are free for dinner tonight, I'd like to take you out," he offered.

She wasted no time in accepting. "Fine. Did you fly or drive?"

Her direct response was catching. "I drove." Nate didn't add that before he saw her, he intended to exchange his faithful vehicle for the SUV he'd been considering for some time.

"Good. Pick me up at seven. You obviously have my address."

Nate received the distinct impression she was about to hang up. "Do you have a preference in restaurants? We probably need a reservation."

"If seafood is acceptable to you, I'll contact Ivar's Salmon House."

Nate raised an eyebrow in amusement. Evidently Ms. Carolyn Sheffield was one independent lady. "Thanks. It sounds good. I'll see you at seven." He hung up, wondering if his plan to admit his true identity, in hopes of enlisting her support, was really such a good idea. His hostess-to-be sounded formidable. He grinned. It would take more than a formidable aunt to keep him from winning Emily Ann Carr. If, of course, Emily was willing to be won. He quickly pushed the thought aside.

The afternoon that Nate had expected to drag by until time to meet Carolyn Sheffield, actually flew past in the

sights and sounds of the celebrating city. Beautifully decorated streets and stores and laughing shoppers. Joyous music
by sidewalk carolers and loudspeakers. Bells being rung by
those who cheerfully donated time to don Santa Claus suits
and man a multitude of Salvation Army kettles that would
help provide for the needy. Tantalizing aromas from dozens
of ethnic restaurants, reminding passers-by of the rich cul-
tural diversity of the "City on the Sound."

Nate thoroughly enjoyed it all. After selecting, purchasing,
and taking possession of a dark red SUV, he hurried back to
his hotel and dressed as carefully as if he were being presented an award. He had a feeling nothing would get by his
dinner date.

He was right. Instead of saying "hello" or "good evening"
when she opened the front door of her home and allowed
him to step into the tastefully decorated foyer, she bluntly
inquired, "Just why did you ask me to dinner, Mr. Alexander?"

Nate felt impaled by her steely gaze. "N. Alexander is actually my pen name," he blurted out. "My real name is Nathan
Alexander Hamilton. I went to school with Em'ly Ann."

Carolyn Sheffield looked at him with intelligent blue eyes.
She said nothing, but Nate recognized that she was sizing
him up with the scrutiny of a father whose sixteen-year-old
daughter was going on her first date. "And she doesn't know."

Nate met her gaze unflinchingly. "No. It started as a joke.
It isn't a joke now. God and Em'ly Ann willing, I intend to
court and marry her."

A twinkle crept into Carolyn Sheffield's eyes, as unexpected
as a party hat on top of snowcapped Mount Rainier. "So, did
you come for my blessing?"

Nate suddenly found himself liking the straight-speaking,
diminutive woman. "No, but now that I've met you, I'd like
to have it."

A quick smile did wonders to warm her stern face. "I'm

not the best person to ask about courting and marrying. I strongly suggest you have this discussion with my niece."

"I intend to. May I accompany you to the airport to meet Em'ly Ann's plane?"

"You can do better than that." She scowled. "Our law offices have been a madhouse lately. Deadlines galore. I need to go in tomorrow morning, long enough to make sure everything's in order before the holidays." The twinkle returned to her eyes. "Besides, if you plan to tell Emily who you are as bluntly as you told me, you don't need a third-party witness."

Nate couldn't help laughing, although his heartbeat quickened at the thought of meeting Emily alone—except, of course, for a multitude of other incoming passengers and their waiting families. He held out his hand. "Thank you, Ms. Sheffield. If all goes well, I hope to someday call you Aunt Carolyn."

The older woman reverted to her usual pseudocynical self. "Perhaps you should break the news to Emily before you count that chicken. . . . Now tell me, are we standing here all night, or are we going to eat? I'm starving!"

Two hours later, following an excellent dinner, Nate dropped Carolyn Sheffield off at her home. "Has Em'ly Ann changed much?" he inquired before leaving. "Will I recognize her?"

"You'll recognize her" was Carolyn Sheffield's enigmatic reply. "Thank you for dinner. Goodnight." She closed the door with resounding finality.

Nate chuckled all the way back to his hotel. If there were more women like Carolyn Sheffield, the world would be a better, more forthright place!

❧

The next morning dawned clear and special—a perfect Seattle winter day. Mount Rainier reigned over the city like a benevolent monarch. Puget Sound shimmered with golden, dancing motes of light. The cries of seagulls joined with the deeper tones of ferryboats plying their trade between the city and nearby islands. Nate Hamilton drove to the airport in a world filled with sunlight and holiday spirit. He found a space in the parking garage and hurried to the terminal. Too bad he couldn't watch Emily Ann's plane come in. Since the tragic events of September 11, 2001, only bona fide passengers could go beyond the security-check stations.

The flight was on time. Nate headed for the baggage-claim area. Carolyn Sheffield had told him to meet Emily there. It felt like an eternity before a trickle of passengers became a steady stream waiting for their baggage. The stream dwindled to a trickle. It ceased. Nate's spirits sank. Had Emily Ann decided not to come?

A few minutes later, a slim woman in a navy blue suit and fetching red scarf appeared. A few silver threads enhanced her brown hair. Her blue eyes looked enormous and a bit frightened as she scanned the baggage area.

Relief flooded through Nate. Except for being more attractively dressed than she used to be in junior high, Emily Ann Carr was simply a grown-up version of his long-lost friend. He should have known she would be the same sweet girl, only older.

❧

Emily Carr gripped her carry-on bag and scanned the baggage area. Where was Aunt Carolyn? She had to be there. Aunt Carolyn was never late for anything. Had she been held up in holiday traffic? If so, she would arrive fuming. Well, there was nothing for Emily to do but claim her suitcase and wait. Emily glanced right again, then left. Still no sign of her aunt.

A tall, handsome man with dark, silver-edged hair stared at her from across the room. Emily wrinkled her forehead, wondering who he resembled. She didn't know anyone in

Seattle but her aunt. Yet his twinkling dark eyes stirred memories and reminded Emily of something pleasant. She glanced at him again, wishing Aunt Carolyn would come. The man was coming her way. What if he spoke to her? Emily took a deep breath. If the man bothered her, she could always summon security.

A final stride brought the stranger to within a few feet of the suitcase Emily had retrieved and parked at her feet. She looked up, prepared to freeze him with a glare, call for help, or both.

The stranger held out a strong hand. His gaze never left Emily's face. When she merely stared at him, he asked in a deep voice, "Don't you know me, Em'ly Ann? You used to." A mischievous look crept into the dark eyes. A smile spread across his face. "Can you still spell *atrocious* and *pretentious?* I never did learn."

Childhood scenes replaced the present: A schoolroom. A shy girl promoted to an Advanced Language Arts class. A friendly boy who turned to her for help.

"Nathan?" she whispered. "Nathan Hamilton?"

He raised his hand. "Present."

She blinked and tried to collect her wits. "This *is* a coincidence! What are you doing here?"

"Meeting you. Your Aunt Carolyn had to go into her office for a short time. I said I'd be happy to pick you up."

His irresistible grin plucked at Emily's heartstrings. She shook her head. Why should this chance meeting with a childhood friend leave her breathless? "How do you know Aunt Carolyn?" she demanded. "Where is Mr. Alexander?"

All traces of mirth left Nate's face. A wistful expression crept into his eyes. "Right here, Em'ly Ann—come to spend Christmas with you."

Emily felt more confused than ever. Her head spun. Had Aunt Carolyn secretly arranged for Nathan to join them, in an effort to spare Emily's feelings when she met Mr. Alexander's fiancée? If so, how had she been able to track him down? How would she even know about Nathan Hamilton? Emily had never shared her girlish admiration. "I–I don't understand," she stammered.

"It's really quite simple, Em'ly Ann. I write and publish as N. Alexander." Nate gathered up her luggage and laughed. "That's the surprise I mentioned in my letter. I'm amazed you never caught on, after all the misspellings I put in my letters for clues."

"You're N. Alexander? That's your surprise?" Emily went from despair to joy. "I thought he was—you were—bringing a fiancée. You know, the woman in the picture." The next instant she'd have given her inheritance to recall the words. Her face scorched with embarrassment. Nate was sure to laugh. When he did, she would march to the nearest ticket counter, obtain the earliest reservation possible, and fly back to Oregon where she belonged.

Nate looked puzzled, but at least he didn't laugh. "Fiancée?" Understanding crept into his dark eyes. "I sent the picture to see if you by chance would recognize me after all these years. The couple in the snapshot are my publisher and his wife."

Publisher and wife? Emily's knees threatened to give way in relief.

Nate took her hand and quietly said, "There has never been a fiancée, Em'ly Ann. Sometimes I've wondered why. Now I know." His smile curled into Emily's heart the way Sister Feline curled into her lap: warm, comforting, and filled with the promise that this Christmas would be a holiday to remember.

"We need to go. We don't want to keep your aunt waiting," Nate reminded.

"Does she know who you really are?"

"I told her last night."

Emily burned with curiosity to hear Aunt Carolyn's response, but decided not to ask. Mischief danced in Nate's face, and Emily wasn't sure she could handle her aunt's reaction on top of the shock she had just sustained.

଼ଈ

Christmas Eve and Christmas Day were perfect—from the midnight church service to the wonderful dinner Carolyn provided. Emily wore her new red dress on both occasions. She basked in the frank approval she saw in Nathan's eyes. Aunt Carolyn tactfully arranged their schedule so as to allow Nate and Emily Ann time alone. They discovered they had even more in common than what their correspondence had revealed. The love rooted in mutual admiration from junior high days and nurtured through their letters, burst into full bloom, as pure and beautiful as the ivory poinsettias decorating Carolyn Sheffield's lovely living room.

Their idyll ended far too soon. To Nate's dismay, he received a summons from his New York publisher. Changes in world conditions required significant revisions to *The Overcomer*. An urgent personal meeting was mandatory.

Nate wasn't happy about his impending trip. "I'll come to Alderdale as soon as I can," he promised. "I wanted to drive you home. We have a lot of years to recapture."

"It's probably just as well," Emily told him. A ripple of laughter escaped. "Harriet Taylor might have a heart attack if I came home from Aunt Carolyn's place with a man. Especially when that man is N. Alexander!"

"Always just Nathan or Nate to you," he reminded. His tender expression and farewell kiss made Emily feel young again. She flew home hugging her precious secret so close, the most prying Alderdale gaze could not ferret it out. There would be time enough for an announcement when Nathan came.

nine

A series of complications conspired to keep Nate in New York. Several frustrating weeks passed before he could return. He resented the delays. "Em'ly Ann and I have already spent too much time apart," he brooded. "I want to get this job done and head back to Alderdale." He contrasted his quiet time in Victoria with the rush and hurry of New York City, and shook his head. New York was a wonderful place to visit, but he longed for the Pacific Northwest's green meadows, towering trees, and singing streams.

❧

While Nate restlessly lingered in New York, excitement descended on Alderdale. A widowed missionary arrived to hold a series of meetings in the church. His first glimpse of Harriet Taylor's quiet daughter Amelia evidently stirred a heart that had been lonely far too long, helping him to see Amelia's potential to be his perfect helpmate. Within days, he had won Amelia's love.

Harriet Taylor swelled with pride that her daughter was marrying such a dedicated Christian man, a man who outshone "dear Porter" on all counts. Her pride soon turned to horror. The "dedicated Christian man" not only planned to take Amelia out of Alderdale, but spirit her into overseas mission service in some faraway land!

Harriet flew into a rage that resounded throughout Alderdale. "No daughter of mine is going to spend the rest of her life taking care of heathens in some God-forsaken country," she proclaimed loud and long. "There are plenty of heathens right here in Oregon who need missionaries."

Meek Amelia evidently didn't care to wait and inherit the earth. When Harriet continued to oppose her daughter's marriage, Amelia straightened her backbone and eloped, leaving Harriet aghast—and alone. Some folks said it served her right. Emily felt sorry for her.

The shock of the elopement didn't lessen until Nathan Hamilton, a.k.a. N. Alexander, arrived and placed a diamond solitaire on Emily Carr's ring finger. The expression in his eyes when he knelt in the best marriage proposal tradition and said, "I love you second only to our Master, Em'ly Ann. Will you marry me?" more than compensated for all her years of waiting for "someday."

She threw her arms around him and whispered, "I will" through happy tears, but she couldn't resist adding, "I'll do the invitations. We want to make sure they are spelled right!" Their betrothal kiss was flavored with laughter.

Tongues wagged about the engagement, but in a kindly manner. Most of the townsfolk were happy for Emily. Isaiah Gerard remembered Nathan as a boy. He and his wife promptly installed Nate in their spare room, telling him to "make himself at home" until the wedding.

No one could figure it out, but for some inexplicable reason, Emily's engagement helped restore Harriet Taylor's shaken self-confidence. She immediately sent Herman Dobbs and his children home and began dropping hints that the engagement came about as a result of her efforts on behalf of "dear Emily." Isaiah Gerard rolled his eyes and snorted.

Nate Hamilton found Harriet's antics hilarious. He had developed strong feelings for the gossipy, close-knit little town and had received Sister Feline's acceptance. At their first meeting, she sniffed Nate and promptly climbed into his lap.

❧

Nate decided there was no better place than Alderdale to settle and complete his memoirs. He and Emily Ann could travel yet always have a home base. He secretly planned to have her old home restored while they were on their honeymoon. Emily Ann had been too busy with fall classes and falling in love to begin remodeling.

"Do we have to wait until May to get married?" he implored.

Emily hesitated. "I suppose not, if that's what you want."

The slight hesitancy in her voice made Nate add, "On the other hand, it might be fun to be sweethearts for a few months before we become man and wife."

Emily's radiant face more than repaid his sacrifice.

One afternoon while writing a particularly memorable experience, Nate's laptop froze up. "Great. By the time I take it somewhere for repairs, I'll have lost my train of thought," he grumped. He quickly called Emily Ann. "May I use your computer, if you aren't?"

"Of course. I'm going grocery shopping." The lilt in her voice made Nate smile.

A short time later, he watched her swing down the walk to her gate, happiness evident in every step. He turned to boot up the computer and switch on the printer. A printout lay in the tray. A title, "The Watch Cat," followed by Emily's byline, caught his attention. Sister Feline's blank stare from a nearby chair made Nate feel like a thief, but temptation proved irresistible. So did the story. Every word moved it forward. Nate's memories fled out the open window. He quickly typed the story on a blank document, printed out a copy, and deleted all evidence of his crime. "Stop making me feel guilty," he told the watching Sister Feline. "It's for Em'ly Ann's own good. She hasn't had the courage to show me her stories, so she obviously hasn't submitted them anywhere." He chortled. "Unless I'm badly mistaken, Em'ly Ann Carr is in for a surprise."

The cat slit her eyes, bounded from the chair, and marched out of the room. Nate was left with the distinct feeling Sister Feline wanted no part of his petty larceny!

❧

Spring danced into Alderdale, following a few halfhearted snow flurries that swirled in the air and moved on. Purple and gold crocus circled the big tree that had stood by the Carrs' front gate for generations. Emily confessed to Nathan, "I planted the crocus in our school colors as a sign of loyalty. How fanciful I was in those days!"

His eyes twinkled. "I hope you haven't changed."

She just laughed.

Spring came early to Emily Ann. Days of delight piled on top of each other. The alders, from which the town took its name, clothed their naked limbs with new leaves. Pussy willows discarded their winter-brown coats in favor of soft, silvery jackets. On a long tramp through the woods, Nate cut a great mass of branches for the table in Emily's hall. "They're enough to 'warm the cockles of your heart,' as Mother used to say," he told her.

She smiled up at him. "My mother said that, too." How good to have someone who understood her upbringing, the way of life that was all she'd ever known—and her love for hometown basketball. Her brother David had been too busy for sports, but Nathan Hamilton had played on the junior high team. Emily's girlish heart thrilled with pride over his success, even though she wasn't able to attend many games.

It was a different story when Bill and Danielle reached high school age. Both loved the sport and made the starting teams in their junior and senior years. Like many small towns, basketball was king during the winter months. No NBA team was more loyally supported than Alderdale's high school teams. Win or lose, the townspeople turned out for both home and away games. Even Harriet Taylor always went to the district finals that determined which teams would go to the state tournament. "They are really the only games that count," she'd been heard to say. No amount of explaining a team wouldn't be in the finals without a good season could change her mind.

Emily reveled in the games. All the pent-up longing of not being able to attend regularly during her high school years made her a faithful fan. She cheered with joy and groaned with despair, depending on which team scored. The looks of triumph Bill and Danielle sent to her in the bleachers brought contentment, and the knowledge she was living up to the trust her brother had placed in her.

Now the basketball games took on an added dimension. Entering the gymnasium on Nathan Hamilton's strong arm made up for Emily's years of seeing couples together while she walked alone. Even knowing she was the target of speculation couldn't dim her joy. It sparkled brighter than the diamond in her engagement ring. Her cup of happiness threatened to run over.

One evening Nate reached for her hand and, under cover of the high school band's lively rendition of "Stars and Stripes Forever," whispered, "Em'ly Ann, I'm so glad we decided to wait until May to get married. Not many people are able to reclaim lost opportunities. I never had a high school sweetheart. All this makes me feel like a teenager again, only better. I'm glad God allowed us to find love later in life. No adolescent romance could compare with what we share."

Emily felt flags of color spring to her face. She squeezed his hand and nodded, too filled with emotion to speak. That night, under the watchful gaze of Sister Feline, she wrote in her journal:

Forgive me, Lord, but all this still seems unreal at times. Most unreal of all is realizing You must have been planning this all the time I waited for "someday."

She fell asleep smiling.

❧

After their initial telephone congratulations, Bill and Danielle kept Emily's e-mail busy with further comments. Danielle enthused:

> *It is so romantic! I don't want to wait more than twenty years to get married, but if it were to someone like N. Alexander—woops, Nathan Hamilton—it might not be so bad! I hate to ask, Aunt Emily, but would you be broken-hearted if I don't fly home for the wedding? My course load is so heavy this quarter, I really need the time for study. Besides, that wonderful man of yours promised he would bring you to see me here at the university when you come back to the East Coast on your honeymoon. What do you think?*

Emily wrote back:

> *I think it is romantic, too. Don't worry about not making it for the wedding. We plan to keep it simple, although it will be in the church and I'll wear a white dress. Nathan likes me in white.*

The irrepressible Danielle shot back another message.

> *I certainly hope he likes you in other colors, as well!*

Nate laughed when Emily read him her niece's comment. "I love you in any color." His eyes twinkled. "Especially in that red dress you wore at Christmas. Oh, and the lavender dress with the lace collar. You wore it to church last Sunday."

Emily suppressed a telltale gasp. Someday she would confess to Nathan the unworthy reason she'd purchased the lavender dress. Not now. It meant opening freshly healed wounds, something Emily didn't want to do in the midst of their joy.

Bill sent a different type of e-mail message in response to Emily's request that he either be Nathan's best man or serve in place of Emily's father and give her away.

"Sorry, Aunt Emily. If Mr. Hamilton wants me for his best man, I'll be happy to serve. But if you think I'm going to give you away, forget it. I'll be happy to walk you down the aisle, although it seems more appropriate for Isaiah Gerard to do that. No way am I giving my Aunt Emily away to anyone!" Bill added a postscript:

In other words, your fiancé can be part of our family, but he can't take you away from Danielle and me.

Nate grinned, picked up the phone, and got Bill on the line. He mimicked Bill's ultimatum. "No way am I going to take Em'ly Ann away from anyone. If I didn't love her to distraction, which I do, I'd be tempted to marry her just to get a nephew and niece. I don't have a single, solitary living relative. You're stuck with me, Bill. By the way, can I count on your being my best man?"

He held out the phone so Emily could hear Bill's laugh, followed by a hearty, "Sure. If you can put up with Danielle and me, we can put up with you! What do you want us to call you?" He laughed again. "It sounds like there are plenty of choices."

"Nate works for me." Nathan cradled the phone. His dark eyes shone with mischief. "Having those two for relatives is going to be great. We'll get along fine. They remind me a lot of the way I used to be." He grinned.

"And still are?" Emily challenged.

The grin widened. "I'm working on it. Say, what do you think of Bill's idea about Isaiah Gerard? I didn't say anything earlier, but he has dropped a couple of broad hints."

"They couldn't be as obvious as the hints in a certain letter I received before Christmas," she teased. When a gleam came into Nathan's eyes, she hastily added, "Not that I minded.

Let's go ask Isaiah. His wife volunteered to play the organ."

The gleam deepened. "We could ask Harriet Taylor to sing," Nate suggested. "Maybe your other fiancé would like to come. Isaiah told me about him."

Emily refused to be baited. "He's long gone, thank goodness." She shuddered. "If I thought Herman Dobbs would show up at our wedding, I'd insist we elope!"

Nate put his arms around her and rested his chin on top of her head. "I doubt that will be necessary. Isaiah says he hasn't seen 'hide nor hair of him' for weeks."

He spoke too soon. After making highly satisfactory wedding arrangements with the Gerards, Nathan and Emily Ann came face to face with her nemesis in the middle of Main Street. His five children surrounded him, and Harriet Taylor was heading toward them with the flat-footed grace of a racing turtle. Heads turned. Emily wanted to sink through the pavement with embarrassment.

Harriet's voice preceded her down the street. "What are you doing here, Herman?" she demanded. "If I've told you once, I've told you a dozen times. It isn't proper for you to be bothering Emily, now that she's promised to Mr. Alexander."

Emily could hardly believe what she was hearing. Harriet Taylor, championing her in front of the listening town?

Herman gave his cousin-in-law a black look. "Mr. Alexander, is it! Don't make me laugh. Underneath that fancy name is plain old Nate Hamilton."

Nate gave him a sunny smile. "That's right. How are you, Mr. Dobbs?"

"Mister nothing. Herman is good enough for me, not like some folks who go sashaying around under an alias."

Alias! Was Herman Dobbs so dumb he didn't know what a pen name was? Emily struggled not to laugh. With Herman in this mood, things could turn ugly.

The wannabe suitor's face contorted into a sneer. "Just

'cause you're some fancy book writer doesn't give you the right to steal my woman. I'm as good a man as you are any day. What do you have that I don't?"

Emily's heart skipped a beat. She felt the muscles of Nathan's arm tense, then relax. The twinkle she loved sprang into his eyes.

Please, God, let his sense of humor get us out of this humiliating mess.

Nate pulled himself to full height and smiled. "I have Em'ly Ann," he said quietly. The next moment, his jaw set. His eyes flashed, but not with fun. The only time Emily had ever seen him like this was more than thirty years earlier. Nathan had caught the school bully picking on a smaller child. Emily Ann had held her breath then, just as she did now.

Nathan's ringing voice dripped icicles. It could be heard the length of Main Street. "Get this, Dobbs. Em'ly Ann has never been 'your woman.' She never will be. If you ever again show up at her home, I'll see that you're arrested for trespassing!"

Herman Dobbs and his children left town the same day.

❧

On Valentine's Day, Emily received several gifts from Nathan. First, the largest heart-shaped box of chocolates she'd ever seen, complete with an old-fashioned paper lace frill and an enormous satin bow. Emily had to shoo Sister Feline away to keep her from chewing on the decorations.

Next came flowers. Emily felt her mouth drop open when Nathan slipped outside and returned with a duplicate of the bouquet she had labeled a "complete garden" months earlier. Mirth bubbled up inside her and she blurted out, "I nearly threw the other bouquet into the street. I thought they had come from Herman Dobbs!"

"You did?" Nate stared at her. "What stopped you?"

Emily wiped away tears. "I decided they were originally God's flowers, and once delivered, they were mine." She breathed in the bouquet's fragrance and continued. "I also wondered if he sent me a copy of *Little Women* but decided it wasn't logical."

"Did it look like this?" Nate lifted the beribboned cover from a box. A leather-bound edition of *Little Men* had *Emily Ann Carr* engraved in gold letters on it.

Her heart thumped, and she reverently lifted the book from its box. "So it was you all the time! How did you know Louisa May Alcott is one of my favorite authors?"

Nate looked sly. "I remember a lot of things from Mrs. Sorenson's class." It was the only explanation he would give.

When Emily reluctantly laid aside her presents, Nate said, "I have one more gift for you, except you don't get the best part of it yet." He handed her a single page on letterhead from his publishing company.

Dear Mr. Alexander,

Thank you for submitting Ms. Emily Carr's story, The Watch Cat. We are as impressed with her work as you obviously are. Does Ms. Carr have other animal stories? If so, we would like to see them as soon as possible. Should we find them as well-written and entertaining as this sample story, we can certainly find a place for them on our children's book list. Thanks again.

"I don't understand," Emily faltered. "How did they get my story?"

Nate dug the toe of a well-polished shoe into the carpet and looked shamefaced. He resembled a small boy caught in mischief. "The day I used your computer, I found a copy printed out." He told how he read it, then rekeyed it back into her computer and made a second copy before deleting the story. "Sister Feline made me feel guilty," he admitted with a quick glance at the cat. "She walked out. I interpreted that as a refusal to condone my misdemeanor."

Sister Feline yawned and looked bored.

Nate grimaced and told Emily Ann, "I was afraid you'd never get around to showing me your stories. I also knew you didn't have the self-confidence to submit them. I considered waiting until our wedding day to give you the letter, but we can't stall the publisher until we get home from our honeymoon. He wants your stories now."

Emily wrapped her arms around him. "I never dreamed the autumn of my life would be the best season of all," she whispered.

"Our winter will be even better," Nathan promised.

&

February bowed out with the Alderdale basketball team losing at the district tournament but vowing to win the following year. In early March, Emily found the old saying "The course of true love never runs smooth," couldn't be more true. Just when everything seemed perfect, a mixed blessing arrived. Reviewers were heralding Nathan's upcoming novel, *The Overcomer*, as his finest. He received a flood of invitations to speak.

Emily was torn between pride in the man she loved and wishing she could have a little more time for him to be "just hers." While she admired "N. Alexander," Nate Hamilton was the boy who captured her heart and kept it. What price would fame demand of them? Qualms concerning her ability to be the wife of someone in the limelight increased when Nathan reluctantly agreed to be the keynote speaker at a Portland convention, where he was to be honored.

"You'll go with me, of course," he told her. A wide grin reminded her of the boy still lurking inside him. "I can hardly wait to have you in the center of the front row."

Emily cringed at the idea. She, appear in front of hundreds of people who had come to see N. Alexander? She opened her lips to refuse but was silenced by Nathan's wistful remark:

"I used to envy those who had someone they loved sitting in the audience."

That evening, Emily wrote in her journal:

> Galatians 5 says longsuffering is a fruit of the spirit, Lord.
> I'm sure Paul didn't mean what I'm feeling, but please, help
> me make it through this ordeal.

Despite her prayer and the confidence inspired by the red dress that Nate insisted she wear, Emily trembled when he seated her in the front row of the large hall then walked to the stage with the convention chairman. Only a few feet of space separated her from her fiancé, yet every glowing word of the introduction made Emily aware of a great gulf widening between them. A quick glance around brought no reassurance. The crowd had not come to see her beloved Nathan, but one of the leading Christian authors in the world. Who was Emily Ann Carr to try and become part of his life? She could almost hear his fans say, "With a world filled with women from which to choose, why on earth did N. Alexander marry such a nobody?"

ten

N. Alexander stepped to the microphone and waited for the audience's enthusiastic reaction to the convention chairman's introduction to subside. Yet it was Nathan Hamilton, not N. Alexander, who looked down into the face of his beloved. He saw the shadow in her expressive blue eyes, the way her gloved fingers interlaced. In a heartbeat, he recognized her distress—and the cause. Long accustomed to the glare of publicity, he'd never considered what this first public appearance with him would mean to Emily. She looked so fragile and vulnerable, he wanted to leave the speaker's platform and go reassure her.

He couldn't do it. In fairness to the crowd that had gathered to hear him speak, he must carry out his part of the program.

When there's no way out, there's always a way up.

Nate mentally cheered. Of course! It wouldn't be hard, either. He had given up speaking from notes years ago. No one knew what he had planned to say. He felt a grin begin and held up his hand for silence. The applause ceased. A final cheer echoed and died. Nathan began to speak.

"I'm not going to tell about the years of struggle I experienced before God opened doors for success. I'm not going to review previous books or preview *The Overcomer,* which will be published in a few months. You can go to the Internet and read all that on my publisher's Web site." He chuckled. "Our publicist does it better than I do anyway!"

Laughter rippled through the audience, a sure sign all were with him.

Nate waited, gaze directed at Emily Ann, who had leaned forward in her seat. Her eyes no longer held a shadow. A tentative smile rested on her lips. Nathan reluctantly tore his attention away from her and swept the audience with a glance.

"Remember when stories began 'Once upon a time' and ended with 'they lived happily ever after'? I'd like to share such a story with you. Once upon a time in a small Oregon town named Alderdale, a boy in a junior high school Advanced Language Arts class dreamed of one day becoming an author. The boy and his classmates had two things of immeasurable value: their teacher and a young girl who had been put in their class because of her intelligence and writing ability. I'm sorry to say it, but we didn't appreciate either Mrs. Sorenson or the newcomer as much as we should have."

Nate sent a quick look at Emily. The blaze of happiness in her eyes and the flare of red in her cheeks made her more beautiful than he had ever seen her. He thanked God that she was here with him and would be for the rest of their lives.

Emily Ann has always been with you, a small voice reminded, *waiting to break free from her chrysalis and into your life like a gorgeous butterfly.*

Exhilarated by the prospect of those years ahead, Nathan went on. "The Bible tells us it is good to confess our sins." He leaned forward and said in a stage whisper, "Don't tell anyone, but I am a terrible speller. I always have been. Two factors made things even worse when I was in school. First, this was BSC—Before Spell Check. Second, and contrary to good writing rules, if I could find a big word, I used it." The audience gasped, then broke into a group laugh.

Nate couldn't remember a time when he'd enjoyed giving a presentation more. "My young classmate saved my skin. If there were words she couldn't spell, they probably weren't in the dictionary." Remembrance stole into his voice. "She also encouraged me more than she, or I, knew at the time. Although she was too shy to say much in words, her eyes lighted up when I read what I considered to be masterpieces in class. Her expression silently shouted, 'You can do it. I believe in you.'"

The silence of the crowd paid homage to the girl in Nathan's story. He cleared his throat and continued. "My family and I left Alderdale at the end of that school term, but I never forgot my faithful friend." He chuckled. "Especially when I hit Spell Check!"

A swell of understanding rose and fell. When it ended, Nathan changed from lighthearted to a serious tone. He outlined his feeling that God was beckoning him to something in addition to writing. "Kipling called it God's 'everlasting Whisper,' the call that comes to those who listen," he explained.

The audience sat spellbound as he related how he began an odyssey to discover what was hidden, lost, and waiting. "I decided to write my memoirs, to reach deep into my past and find the boy buried deep under layers of years and success. I also sought God with my whole heart and listened for His whisper. I felt His presence in my life stronger than I'd experienced in years."

Nate paused, reached into his pocket, and unfolded a crumpled page. He looked down at Emily, whose eyes opened wide. "A letter concerning *The Seeker* helped give my life and search perspective. It ended with these words: 'Whether this book wins awards, as some of your other titles have done, isn't nearly as important as the encouragement it offers to those bound by life's "everydayness," as well as by major obstacles.

"'I am sure many readers will be blessed by the example your courageous hero set. Yet if I were the only one, *The Seeker* still needed to be written.'"

Nathan paused and waited for the obstruction in his throat to clear. When he could speak coherently again, he quietly said, "The letter came from a woman I hadn't seen in more than thirty years. She had no idea N. Alexander was the boy she'd helped with his spelling in junior high!"

The audience straightened, as if jolted by his words. Some started to clap, but Nathan raised his hand for silence and resumed his narrative. "I decided to learn more about the writer. I began to correspond with her, always as N. Alexander. There had been no time for love in my life and travels, but as the weeks passed, I came to care deeply for my new correspondent. She still didn't know who I was."

He smiled down at the center of the front row of seats. "I won't go into the details of our first meeting. It's enough to say that my memoirs will have a 'happily ever after' ending." He left the platform, marched to the front row, and escorted his fiancée to the microphone. "I am proud to announce that my childhood sweetheart, although I didn't recognize she was that until recently, has agreed to become my wife. I give you Em'ly Ann Carr, the love of my life and a blessing from my heavenly Father."

૨૦

It felt like an eternity to Emily Ann before the standing ovation ended. Nate kept her hand in his and laughingly answered or fended off questions from the audience. Emily tried to concentrate but failed miserably. All she could think about was the look of love in Nathan's shining dark eyes and the high tribute he had publicly given her. She would never again need to feel unworthy. She was acceptable in Nathan's sight—and God's. It was all that mattered.

The crowning moment of the event came unexpectedly and after Nate received his award. The crowd had dispersed, except for a few stragglers expressing congratulations.

"Well done, Nathan. I knew you could succeed if you tried

hard enough," a familiar voice said. "Hello, Emily. It looks like the Spell Check on Nate's computer is being replaced."

They turned toward a beaming white-haired lady. Emily gave a happy cry. "Mrs. Sorenson!"

"None other." Their old teacher's laugh took Emily Ann back to the classroom. "I see you haven't forgotten *The Explorer*," she told Nate. "If you had used it in your N. Alexander books, I'd have suspected who you really were. I'm proud of you." She turned to Emily. "What about you? Were you able to continue writing?"

She shook her head. "Mostly journals."

"Don't be modest, Em'ly Ann," Nathan objected. "My publisher is impressed with a children's story she recently revised. It may become the core story of a book."

"What wonderful news!" Mrs. Sorenson exclaimed. "By the way, am I invited to your wedding?"

"If you promise not to critique it," he teased. They parted in a wave of excitement and with the knowledge that they would meet again soon.

ಏ

April came to Alderdale. March storms were replaced by gentler, rain-filled breezes that kissed blooming trees and flowers. Emily Carr found herself repeating Song of Solomon 2:11–12: "For, lo, the winter is past, the rain is over and gone; the flowers appear on the earth; the time of the singing of birds is come, and the voice of the turtle [dove] is heard in our land."

Nathan always responded with the last sentence of the next verse: "Arise, my love, my fair one, and come away," followed by a mischievous grin.

With each passing day, Emily and Nathan's love deepened. With each passing day, Emily Ann gave thanks to God for the wonder Nate brought into her life. A simple walk beside a brook or through a meadow became an adventure. The first time Sister Feline accompanied them, curled around Nathan's neck like a black-and-white muffler, Emily Ann laughed until her sides ached. The cat purred and looked smug. From then on, she trotted to the door and meowed every time Emily put on a jacket.

Emily had always loved the woods. She had sought refuge from heartache in their depths countless times. Now the thrill of sharing a place she cherished with the man she loved enhanced every turn of the trail.

"Even though there are a lot of changes, it still feels the same," Nathan said one afternoon, when the forest's invitation to explore proved too alluring and took him from his memoirs. "I knew I missed it, but I didn't realize how much until I came back. Does that make sense?"

"Yes." Emily felt herself blush. "That's the way it was when you came back into my life." She adjusted the crown of leaves he had made and placed on her head. "I just didn't want to admit it for fear you wouldn't. . ." Her voice trailed off.

"I understand." Nate's eyes glowed with tenderness. "I'm glad that's all behind us." He put a kiss in her palm, closed her fingers over it, then curled her hand in his. "Let's never have any secrets between us, all right?"

"Right." She smiled, feeling happiness rise from the toes of her sturdy walking shoes to the leafy crown.

Nate completed his memoirs near the end of April. Emily Ann proofed them. She marveled at the high place he had given her and secretly prayed, *Lord, please help me become what Nathan thinks I already am.* Her children's stories were finished and submitted. Emily alternated between believing Nate's prediction that they would be published and feeling he was prejudiced.

May 1 crept into Emily's pale green and white bedroom on silent feet. She awakened troubled. Not with feelings of inferiority, thank goodness, but a more practical dilemma. Only two weeks remained before the wedding, and she still hadn't found a satisfactory wedding present for Nathan. When she timidly asked him what he wanted, he smirked and said, "You!" Her persistent inquiries as to what he really wanted brought the same unhelpful answer. He had relented and told her his gift was to restore the old home. What could she offer him in return?

A daring thought came. *Give Nathan a part of yourself. The thing only you, God, and Sister Feline know exists: your journals.*

Emily immediately rejected the idea. "I can't," she whispered, so low, Sister Feline didn't stir from her slumbers at the foot of the bed. "It would make me too vulnerable."

Nothing else you possess is so fitting.

The silent reminder haunted her day and night. A week before the wedding, Emily packed her journals in chronological order, put a bow on the large box, and quietly gave her innermost self to Nathan one sunny afternoon. Then she fled. From the shelter of a curtain, she watched him walk down the rose-strewn path to her gate, carrying the heavy box. For the first time since she was ten years old, she had no journal in which to write, or the incentive to start a new one. Had she made a terrible, irrevocable mistake?

The memory of Nathan's face that day in the woods when he said, "Let's never have any secrets between us, all right?" shimmered in Emily's tear-filled eyes. She hadn't been thinking of the journals then, just the joy of being loved.

Peace came softly. Yet anticipation and dread for the moment when she would face her fiancé, knowing he was aware of every secret corner of her life, mingled. Evening fell. She and Sister Feline sought out the porch swing, half-hidden by the clusters of roses climbing the porch posts.

Ringing footsteps heralded Nathan's approach. Emily felt powerless to rise and go to him, as she normally did. The gate opened. He walked up the path, up the steps. An expression of humility, awe, and yearning blended with inexpressible love. "My dear Em'ly Ann." He held out his arms, obviously unable to say more.

She unceremoniously dumped her cat onto the porch floor. She barely heard Sister Feline's infuriated "Meowrr!" Straight as a homing pigeon, Emily Ann flew into Nathan's waiting arms.

❧

The clump of solid footsteps, the rustle of skirts, and the heavy scent of perfume heralded the first guest to arrive at Emily Carr's wedding in the small church her family had attended for several generations.

Harriet Taylor—tall, spare, and gimlet-eyed—marched down the center aisle and surveyed the quiet, dimly lit chapel with satisfaction. No one here yet. Good. She did like to be first and have her choice of seats. She reached the reserved area in the front and ruthlessly tore free the guarding ribbon. After all, she *was* Emily Carr's second cousin twice removed.

❧

Carolyn Sheffield observed Harriet's entrance from the one-way window of the cry room at the back of the chapel. She remembered the altercation at Bill's wedding and grimaced, but behind Emily Ann's back. No unpleasant memory should mar her niece's wedding day. Besides, Harriet without Amelia seemed pathetic.

"So much for having a small wedding," Carolyn told Emily.

"I know." Emily Ann's face shone like one of the flowers in her bridal bouquet, a smaller replica of the others Nathan had given her. "I couldn't draw the line." She paused. "Aunt Carolyn, you don't feel bad about not giving me away, do you? Isaiah Gerard really wanted to do it."

"*I?*" Carolyn sniffed. "You'll never catch *me* walking down a church aisle in a wedding."

"Never say never," Emily teased. "Look at me."

"I've got you by a good twenty years," her aunt reminded.

"Are you ready? It's almost time." She surveyed her niece with satisfaction. "That white silk and the circlet of flowers with the short veil are perfect."

"I hope Nathan thinks so." Emily fingered the rich folds of her skirt.

"He will." Carolyn checked her watch. "Isaiah is waiting for you, and it's time for me to go be seated." Her fingers pressed Emily's. Affection softened her voice. "You look lovely. Your mother would be so proud." She slipped out before Emily could reply, leaving the door open.

Emily watched her aunt take Bill's arm and walk to the front row. Her throat tightened. If only Mother could be here today. Mother and Father and David. Their precious faces passed through Emily's mind in a kaleidoscope of memories. She was thankful that nothing could dim those memories.

Isaiah Gerard's soft, "Em'ly Ann?" recalled her to the present. This day must not be spoiled by looking back. "Remember Lot's wife," Emily told herself. She laughed, stepped from the cry room, and firmly closed the door behind her.

The fragrance of candles and roses greeted Emily—roses from Emily's garden, lovingly arranged by the churchwomen. A beaming Isaiah Gerard offered his arm. The wedding march began. Approving faces—even Harriet Taylor's—turned toward Emily. Mrs. Sorenson caught her attention and slowly winked. Emily took a deep, tremulous breath. Her *someday* had really come. Or was it all just a lovely dream, a dream from which Sister Feline's cool nose and reaching paw would awaken her? The need for reassurance made Emily's lace-clad fingers tremble on Isaiah Gerard's strong arm.

Did he sense what she was feeling? Perhaps, for he patted her hand with his free one, then whispered so low that no one but she and God could hear, "Don't be nervous, Em'ly Ann. Look at Nate."

She raised her head and gazed at the tall, handsome man waiting for her at the altar. A quick mist blurred her vision but could not dim the blaze of love and admiration in Nathan Hamilton's unguarded dark eyes. His look of mingled pride and humility swept lingering doubts away forever. The wedding was real and the love she and Nate shared would be theirs for as long as they both should live. Emily Ann tightened her grasp on Isaiah's arm and proudly stepped forward to meet her *someday*.

Three things about Emily's wedding registered more deeply than all the rest. First, Nathan's ringing, "I, Nathan, take thee, Em'ly Ann." Next, the irrepressible mischief in his eyes when he slipped a gold band on her ring finger. Finally, an incident following the simple reception in the fellowship hall that she and Nathan had chosen over some elaborate affair.

"Don't forget to throw your bouquet," Nate told her when they reached the sidewalk in front of the church.

"I hate to give it up, even though you had it reproduced in silk," she said with regret; but she obediently turned. Arm high, she gave her flowers a mighty fling.

The bouquet sailed high over the heads of those gathered, as if ignoring the bevy of eager, reaching hands in order to seek out a more worthy recipient. It landed in a pair of arms automatically flung up in self-protection against the flowery missile.

Carolyn Sheffield's arms.

Silence gave way to cheers. Nate hurried Emily into his waiting car. "Now's our chance to get away." He laughed uproariously. "I suspect this is the first time your aunt has ever been shocked speechless. Did you see her face?"

Emily Ann burst into giggles. "That's not all I saw!" Tears of mirth streamed. "Harriet Taylor stared at Aunt Carolyn as if she'd received a sign from heaven." Emily wiped her eyes.

"I hope she doesn't start plotting to marry off Aunt Carolyn!"

"Carolyn Sheffield can take care of herself," Nathan reminded. He put the car in gear and grinned across at Emily in the endearing way that made him so boyish and beloved. "Time to start our honeymoon, Em'ly Ann." Laughter twinkled in his dark eyes. "Just one thing. How do you spell *stupendous, exhilarating,* and *worth waiting for?*"

Part 2: Carolyn
eleven

Anticipation buzzed through the Seattle law firm of Jensen, Cook, and Franz like power lines against a high wind. Carolyn Sheffield was not immune. Fifty years at the firm and she still felt the Bonus Day butterflies. August 1 was a day that rivaled Christmas in the minds of the 152 firm employees.

Carolyn chided herself. Fifty years of August firsts at the firm, and she was still acting as if it were her first prom.

She knew the routine by heart. Mr. Jensen would gather all the partners in the boardroom. The firm's annual profits would be unveiled. Then each partner would leave with an envelope. Not just any envelope: The Envelope. Each employee would pretend not to look as it passed office door after office door. But the secret held within was too powerful. Invariably, eyes would be drawn upward. They had to look. As if looking would reveal contents. Hushed whispers speculated. Fifteen thousand dollars, twenty thousand—could it be thirty thousand dollars? Finally, the opening and grand announcement. The Bonus amount each employee would receive, and greater still, the Employee of the Year.

"Employee of the Year," Carolyn murmured in hushed tones, as if saying it too loudly would detract from the reverence of the title. Sixty-nine years of life, and she still had seen no greater honor. Past winners were treated like royalty. Whispers of awe and respect followed them.

Carolyn sighed. "Winning that honor would make me the

happiest woman in the world. I don't suppose You'd like to help out on this one?" she whispered with a heavenward glance.

The jarring ring of the fax jolted her out of her blissful daydream. "You silly old woman," she said, shaking her head. "A grown professional paralegal dreaming like a schoolgirl."

Forcing her mind back to reality, she tackled the large pile of papers next to her with gusto. She had work to get done, and daydreaming was not going to make the pile go away. The red numerals on the clock teased her. "One second, two seconds, three seconds," each flash of the dots seemed to say.

This is ridiculous, she decided, turning the clock toward the wall. *Clocks cannot speak—and two o'clock will get here a lot faster if I don't count the seconds.*

The day droned mercilessly on. Carolyn unsuccessfully tried to find ways to concentrate on something other than the magical hour. But the Kelly brief, the Lyons motion, and the summons and complaint on Baker fell short of the mark. After three hours of semisustained effort, she managed to make a small dent in the pile, but not without a number of forays into the land of daydreams.

"Carolyn, are you feeling all right?" Her coworker Anna's question pierced her reverie.

"Oh," she replied, looking down at her wringing hands. "It's just a little carpal tunnel syndrome. It will be fine."

"I'm amazed you can still work twelve- to fourteen-hour days." Anna shook her head in disbelief. "Not to mention training all of us youngsters to be acceptable paralegals and attorneys. You know you're the only reason half of the attorneys here keep their jobs. If you weren't walking behind them cleaning up their messes and preparing their briefs, they'd be sunk. I guess that's why you get paid the big bucks. In fact, if I were choosing, without a doubt you'd be the Employee of the Year."

Carolyn looked at the girl. "Well, you know, I just do my

job," she mumbled, not exactly sure how to deal with such complimentary statements.

"Anna's right, you know." Bryant, an associate fresh out of law school, peeked his head around the corner. "We attorneys couldn't do without you; you know more law than the lot of us combined. Besides, what would we do without you telling us how wrinkled our shirts and how atrocious our manners are? You've got *my* vote for Employee of the Year, too."

Carolyn warily looked over her nose at the black-haired charmer and suppressed a grin. "Don't you believe for a second, Mr. Black, that I don't know the game you're playing. I've been around too many years to fall for your line. Your brief is still due on my desk by Friday, and I still do not get your coffee."

Bryant smiled and lifted the five-foot-two-inch, 105-pound object of his teasing off the ground in a boyish hug. "Ah, Carolyn, if I could only find a woman like you my age, I'd be married in a second."

"Bryant married? Now that's a scary thought," Mr. Jensen's administrative assistant Evelyn teased, coming around the corner.

"Hi, Ev." Carolyn smiled. "What are you doing slumming in our department? Don't suppose you want to share any leaks about what's going on behind the conference room's closed doors."

"Carolyn." Evelyn leaned in. "You and I have been here longer than most. You know I would share anything I know with you, but that meeting is as closed as Fort Knox. Jensen even types the agenda himself, on one of those old type-writers. All I know is, I was sent to come get you."

Carolyn's eyebrows furrowed. "Whatever for?"

"I have no idea, unless. . .well, you know the rumors."

"What rumors, Ev?" Bewilderment resounded in her voice. "What on earth are you talking about?"

"Oh, come on, Carolyn, you know you're a shoo-in for Employee of the Year. Everybody knows."

Could it be true? Following Evelyn down the hall, Carolyn felt the blood rushing to her face, coursing with the possibility. *After all this time?*

Memories of the past fifty years came flooding into her mind. Long hours spent at the office. Night and weekend activities sacrificed for pending deadlines. Canceled dates. Broken romances, victims of her desire to be a "working woman." Friendships ruined by lack of time.

Looking back, Carolyn marveled. She had given up so much. Everything, really. Fun. Friendship. A love life. *Love.* The word made her stop short. Experience had taught her that its synonym was *heartbreak.* She was terminally single and glad of it, she reassured herself. *So much gone,* she mused, *but in pursuit of what?*

My career, my dream, she answered quickly. *And now*—she paused, letting the reality soak in—*now I will receive my reward. Carolyn Sheffield, Employee of the Year. It has a nice ring to it.*

"Thank you, Lord," she whispered, surprised at how foreign the words sounded. Could it have been that long since she had prayed? "You really didn't forget me."

The conference-room doors were open when Evelyn and Carolyn arrived. Carolyn caught Evelyn's smile and thumbs-up as she stepped through the marbled doors.

Seated at the head of the table was Mr. Jensen, flanked by rows of dark, expensively-suited attorneys. "Welcome, Carolyn." His gravelly voice echoed in the marbled chamber. "Please sit."

Carolyn gingerly sat on the edge of the velvet chair he indicated. How exactly was one supposed to look when given such an honor, she wondered. Surprised? Elated? Deserving? Cool as a cucumber? Classy? That was it. She would be classy.

Pulling herself out of her internal debate, she caught only part of what Mr. Jensen was saying.

"And so, Ms. Sheffield, we felt we had no choice but to take this course of action. You have served this firm well. We will miss you."

"I'm sorry," Carolyn queried. "Miss me? I don't understand."

"Like I said, our profit earnings came back at a record low this year. A breakdown of the figures shows the revenues from the firm's Personal Injury section failed to cover its costs for the second year in a row. We have no choice but to dissolve the entire section. We won't be doing any more PIs. The existing cases will be farmed out to the other departments to wrap up. Given your longevity, we thought you should be the first to know. I'm sorry, but this is good-bye."

Carolyn blanched. The blood rushed from her face, leaving an expressionless pallor. Numb, she looked around the table at those with whom she had worked. None would meet her gaze. Her legs suddenly seemed like stiff boards. The wooden feeling moved upward.

She stood, aware of only one thing in the room: the door. She had to get to the door. Staring straight ahead, Carolyn walked stiffly out the door, down the corridor, and out into the atypical gray August Seattle day.

twelve

Carolyn Sheffield glared at the face staring back at her from the beveled mirror in her foyer. "Who took my features and gave them to this old woman?" she half-sarcastically remarked.

Moving closer, she examined the lines marking the edges of her face. "Laugh lines," as her ever-optimistic friend Ruth Welch referred to them. Only, unlike Ruth's, the grooves etched in Carolyn's face didn't even hint of a smile, much less a laugh. "Old age breeds character," Carolyn reminded, but failed to convince, herself. "Old age breeds loneliness and ruin" had a much truer ring.

She pulled herself away from the mirror and slumped down in the burgundy Queen Anne chair standing guard in her home's vaulted entryway. Only a few months ago, she had treasured the sun's rays that flooded the foyer through the skylight and glass-paneled doors. Now the autumn light not only revealed every flaw in her sixty-nine-year-old face but also mocked the darkness that permeated her from head to toe. In search of a place more in keeping with her mood, she headed for the living-room sofa, planted herself face down, and covered her head with the throw pillow. Even there, the thoughts she'd been trying to escape since her lay-off two months ago pelted her like icy chunks of hail. *Alone. Old. Worthless. Unemployed.* It didn't matter what politically correct term Jensen, Franz, or whoever else tried to attach— it all boiled down to the same ugly truth. She had been fired! More than fifty years of her life had been devoted to her profession, and it was over. The sacrifices! Sleep. Vacations. Friends. Love. For nothing. How could God let this happen?

Wasn't He supposed to care about her?

The incessant ringing of the doorbell brought a welcome interruption from the company of her own morbid thoughts. *Now, who would have nothing better to do than visit this sorry old woman today?* It was a bit refreshing to know that even her negative alter ego parried in sarcasm. Perhaps the old spitfire Carolyn was down there someplace. *But where?* Carolyn asked herself as she slowly went to greet her semiwelcome caller.

Her hand barely touched the knob before a whirlwind of energy that rivaled the sunlight blew through the door.

"Carolyn, dear, how are you today?" Ruth's arms stretched around her childhood friend in an embrace as warm as fresh cinnamon buns. Just a shade over five-feet-three-inches tall, Ruth's frame softened in all the places Carolyn's angled. Her spunky energy was fueled by a heart that worked on overdrive and a spirit to match. Even long-term acquaintances marveled at the life-long friendship between the two unlikely comrades. Sarcasm and guile were as foreign to Ruth as the high-powered legal career her friend Carolyn had chosen. Ruth's life had been devoted to her family. After her husband, Jim, passed away a decade earlier, she had thrown herself full-time into the charitable work that came so naturally to her. Yet despite their differences, the bond these women forged was unbreakable.

Carolyn avoided her friend's question. "Lemonade or soda?"

"Lemonade, please. Oh, and we have so much to talk over. How about wrestling us up a couple of cookies?" Ruth's concerned gaze wandered over Carolyn's disappearing figure. She remained silent. Years of friendship had taught Ruth the fruitlessness of mothering Carolyn.

Returning with the refreshments, Carolyn seated herself next to Ruth. "Now who are you saving in the world *this* week?"

"I wish I could say you. Carolyn, I'm so worried about you." Ruth's eyes filled with tears. "You have to get out."

Glancing over Carolyn's shoulder to the assortment of delivery and take-out boxes on the kitchen counter, Ruth continued with an uncharacteristic boldness. "From the looks of things, I'd guess it's been at least a week since you've left your house. You're wearing the same ensemble you had on when I saw you last week. And don't forget, honey, I have seen that walk-in closet of yours. I know it isn't because you have a lack of clothing options."

Ruth paused, taking a deep breath. "Carolyn, in the sixty years I've known you I have *never* seen your hair out of place." She ran her hand through her own wayward white locks. Eyes twinkling, she lowered her voice in mock horror. "The style you are sporting today wouldn't even qualify as disheveled. Today your hair looks worse than *mine!*"

Despite her best efforts to be angry at Ruth's interference, Carolyn couldn't help but chuckle. "Well, Ruth, if what you say is true about my hair, I must be in terrible trouble. Worse than yours? It can't be. The horror. The *horror.*"

As the two friends shared a laugh, Carolyn noted how foreign it felt. Had it been that long since she'd laughed aloud? The thought unnerved her a bit. Perhaps there was something to Ruth's concern. Not that she'd ever admit it to her friend, but she had noticed her clothes were hanging loosely on her five-foot-two-inch frame. She hadn't had a lot of impetus to do her hair or choose her clothes lately, either. Carolyn pulled herself away from her reverie and joined Ruth midsentence.

". . .so I thought you would be able to come out with me and celebrate."

"Celebrate? I'm sorry, Ruth; celebrate what again?"

"The Hospital Guild is going to have a fund-raiser for the cancer unit. They are giving me some kind of award for the work I've done with the Guild. Please come. You can support me, and maybe there will be some nice older gentlemen there. . . ."

Carolyn snorted. "Nice older gentlemen. Please. You are talking to the wrong woman. Remember, I'm terminally single and proud of it. I need another bad experience with a man right now about as much as I need a kick in the head. I've told you before, and I'll keep telling you—I don't want to double date, even with you. I certainly don't want to single date. Right now I hate the idea of dates so much, I wouldn't even eat one."

"Now, Carolyn," Ruth gently responded, ignoring her friend's tirade. "How are you going to meet a nice man like your niece Emily did, if you won't even be in the same room with one?" With a wink Ruth added, "I think there are some wonderful older Christian men out there who are just waiting for two almost-seventy-year-old mature and beautiful women to knock their socks off. It might as well be us."

Carolyn rolled her eyes and shook her head. "As usual, my friend, you are ever the optimist. Emily found a wonderful man, that's true; but she's more than twenty years younger than we are, and she was extremely lucky. I'm afraid she pulled the needle out and left us the haystack. I don't know about you, but I have absolutely no interest in hay. And I certainly have no interest in knocking anyone's foot coverings off. I will, however, accompany you to the Guild's fund-raiser."

Carolyn stopped, then teasingly added, "That is, if I can find anything my newly appointed fashion critic will deem suitable for me to wear. *And* if I can get this disheveled mop on my head in order."

Ruth smiled at her friend. "I don't care if you stay in that outfit and don't touch your hair until the fund-raiser night; as long as you are there by my side, I will be thrilled."

As she headed out Carolyn's front door, Ruth smiled and yelled over her shoulder, "But if you want to attract one of those nice men, you might consider a comb and a good launder of those clothes!"

❧

Carolyn glanced in the mirror and brushed down a stray silver-tinged auburn lock before heading out of her bathroom. Not perfect, but presentable. At least more presentable than she had managed in the last couple of months. She had almost called Ruth to back out of attending the fund-raiser, but she couldn't bear to hurt her friend. The familiar sound of Ruth's VW Bug's horn beckoned from the curb. Carolyn hastily grabbed her shawl and headed out the front door.

"Might as well get this over with," she muttered as enthusiastically as if she were heading to her yearly doctor's appointment.

She opened the door and plopped down next to Ruth. The happy chatter from the driver's seat kept Carolyn's mind off the looming evening of fun and festivities. As they pulled into the parking lot, Carolyn comforted herself with the thought that the hospital fund-raising set was usually fairly uninspired: *A couple of appetizers, Ruth's acceptance speech, and I'm out of here.*

Her speculations were rudely interrupted by the faint strains of music. "There must be another group celebrating here as well," Carolyn mentioned to Ruth. Ruth's unusual silence greeted her.

"Ruth?" Carolyn glanced at her friend for an explanation.

Ruth squirmed, looking uncomfortable. "Did I not mention there was square dancing at this event?" Unaccustomed to even a whisper of deception, Ruth's face screamed guilt.

Carolyn bristled. Remembering the importance of the evening for her friend kept her response in check but could not keep the annoyance from her voice. "No. You forgot that little detail."

Ruth looked sideways at her friend. "I'm sorry, Carolyn. When you said you'd come, I was so happy. I only found out yesterday that they were going to have square dancing, and I just couldn't bring myself to tell you. I knew you wouldn't come. Please forgive me." Her soft arms instantly wrapped around her beanpole of a friend.

Carolyn's reticent "You're forgiven" was followed by a spirited, "but don't expect me to dance."

Ruth's face showed she knew better than to push for that.

Carolyn provided a few cursory nods in the direction of the familiar faces she saw, obligingly watched as Ruth's honor was presented, then excused herself to the hall outside the dance floor. Old-fashioned country melodies and the caller's voice squeezed under the door and kept her company in her chair.

Even though she was annoyed, the vision of the hoity-toity, business-suited clan twirling about the floor to a country caller, touched Carolyn's funny bone. Her amusing visions were interrupted by the hall doors brusquely opening. Ruth, red-faced and teary-eyed, rushed past her into the women's restroom.

Carolyn bolted out of her seat and after her friend. Opening the restroom door, she saw Ruth sobbing in a corner chair. Carolyn quickly went to her side, and in an unusual display, wrapped her arms around her dear friend. She said nothing, waiting for her friend's sobs to abate.

After awhile, Ruth's shoulders stopped heaving, and her breathing slowed. "Oh, Carolyn. It was so humiliating. He was in the corner, looking lonely. I thought I'd cheer him up and ask him out on the floor to dance. He said he preferred a woman who made the effort to keep herself fit and would rather stay in the corner than dance with me. Everyone heard." The rendition of the story sent Ruth into a new fit of sobs. "I was just trying to be nice. It was just so humiliating."

Carolyn's ire rose faster than she did, as she stood bolt upright. "Which cad did this to you?"

"I don't know his name. I've never seen him before."

"What did he look like?" Carolyn demanded.

Ruth wiped her eyes. "Well, he was tall—probably six-one. He had that pure white hair. I'd say he was very distinguished-looking—especially in his dark suit. Why, Carolyn? What are you going to do?" Ruth paused, as if considering her own question. Her eyes widened at the determined look on Carolyn's face. "Oh, Carolyn, please. Don't make a scene. I can't bear to show my face out there as it is. I don't want any more attention."

Carolyn's jaw set determinedly. "Ruth, any man who would treat you in such a cruel and heartless way wouldn't hesitate to tread on the feelings of any woman. Maybe a bit of his own medicine will give him pause next time he is asked to dance. I'd say he needs a crash course in Civility 101—and I just happen to know a willing and able teacher." She winked at Ruth to alleviate her friend's fear. "Believe me, my dear, the attention will not be on *you*."

With her parting words, Carolyn headed into the ballroom, armed only with the sketchy description of the offending party provided by her distraught friend. As she entered the dance floor, her gaze was immediately drawn to a tall, distinguished-looking white-haired gentleman who was deep in conversation across the room.

"Doesn't it figure—the best looks in the room wasted on an egoist," Carolyn whispered to herself. "Typical."

She squared her shoulders, straightened up to her full five-foot-two height, and marched across the room with unwavering purpose. Upon reaching the gentleman's elbow, Carolyn grabbed it, forcefully interrupting his conversation.

Surprise resonated on the white-haired man's face. "I'm sorry—do I know you?"

"After this conversation, you are going to wish you didn't," Carolyn responded loudly. "How dare you humiliate and ridicule my friend? You not only lost the opportunity to dance with the most wonderful woman here tonight, but you crushed and embarrassed her. You did not deserve the honor of having her invite you to dance—nor any other lady for that matter. In the future, however, if a lady *is* unfortunate enough to ask you to dance, I suggest you accept. If you choose not to dance with her again, that is your prerogative, but turn her down nicely, quietly, and without destroying her self-esteem. Do you understand? I can guarantee you this: No lady here tonight will be dancing with you if I have any say in the matter."

Carolyn turned abruptly and headed resolutely back across the floor. "Men," she mumbled. "It figures."

When she reached Ruth in the restroom, she managed to paste a smile on her still scorching-hot face. She helped her friend to her feet, wrapped her arm around her shoulders, and headed toward the beckoning exit doors. To Ruth's questioning gaze, Carolyn responded, "Let's just say I'm sure he's grateful that our paths will cross but once in this life." She paused, then punctuated her thought. "Good riddance."

thirteen

Though Carolyn felt like a lamb being led to the Guild-party slaughter, she was forced to admit she was glad Ruth had pressed the issue. The unexpected value of the evening, the opportunity to dress down the debonair Mr. "I only dance with fit women," had ignited a pilot light she had not realized was out. Traces of the old Carolyn began periodically to show up, startling even her.

Carolyn admitted as much to Ruth over hot scones. "I caught a glimpse of my reflection last week in the produce mirror at the grocery. Not that the vegetable-and-fruit-aisle mirror is the most flattering, but I halted in shock and said out loud, "Who is that woman—and what has she done with my hair?"

She paused, looking at Ruth. "Do you realize I hadn't seen my beautician in over half a year? I don't care what the hair-care products promise, eight months of grow-out on this almost seventy-year-old head does *not* look natural."

Ruth clutched her stomach at her friend's comments and gasped. "Oh, Carolyn, stop. I can't laugh anymore. My stomach muscles won't take it." She converted her laugh into a wide smile. "It's so good to have you back, my dear. I've missed that irascible streak."

"Well, I'm not totally back to fighting strength, but I'd say I'm off bed rest. Maybe in time, I will recover." Carolyn paused, ruminating on her own words. "At least the hair's back to normal."

"Speaking of hair," Ruth awkwardly segued, "now that you've got your locks looking so good, wouldn't it be nice to show them off?" She smiled, guilt reverberating off her angelic pink cheeks.

"What now?" Carolyn snorted. "You got another square dance up your sleeve? No, thank you. As much as I appreciate it spurring me out of my blue funk, it was an experience I don't care to repeat in the near future."

Ruth smiled. "No, it's nothing like that. We're just really short on volunteers at the hospital. We could use some help."

"Sorry." Carolyn shook her head. "I don't have the legs for those candy-striper skirts."

Ruth stood and handed Carolyn a Community Memorial badge with her name and *Volunteer* emblazoned in black. "You can wear something from your closet—and this badge. Your first shift is Saturday. You are assigned to the geriatric ward with me. It will be good for you. Besides, you couldn't have a better partner.

"I've got to go deliver dinner to Henry Lamb," she continued. "You know he can't cook a lick, and since Rachel died, he's been thinning out. I'll pick you up Saturday at nine A.M." Ruth's eyes twinkled, and she bustled out the door.

Carolyn sat speechless, staring at the badge. As recognition of what her friend had roped her into dawned, she couldn't help but wryly grin. "Anyone who says that girl doesn't have a manipulative bone in her body doesn't know Ruth Welch like I do. Innocent, my foot. She may talk a sweet streak, but she's a sly one." Looking down at her name badge, she tried the words on for size. "Carolyn Sheffield, Volunteer." Just the thought made her chuckle. "Won't Emily get a kick out of this. I bet she will be as surprised as I am."

By Saturday, Carolyn's surprise had turned to determination. "If I could run a legal firm for decades, I certainly can volunteer at a hospital successfully." Carolyn walked through a two-hour orientation with Ruth and then headed out to take Geriatrics by storm. Even Ruth's questioning gaze couldn't shake Carolyn's confidence.

Carolyn turned down cold Ruth's "Are you sure you don't want me to stay with you for a couple of hours, until you've practiced a bit?"

"Ruth, if I could take orders from a bunch of legal eagles, I can certainly handle the over-seventy crowd's lunch orders. Don't worry; I'll be fine."

Carolyn resolutely marched to the first room and commenced her duties. "Ms. Smith, room 675. She requests meatloaf and potatoes, hold the gravy; apple juice; and whatever the pudding was she had for dinner last night—it was yellow, but she doesn't have a clue what flavor it was. Mr. Johnson, room 652, would like a big bowl of green Jell-O—nothing else." The list proceeded smoothly, as did Carolyn's shift.

Ruth gave Carolyn a thumbs-up and a wink each time she saw her. Toward the end of the shift, Carolyn approached room 643 and knocked lightly. When no one responded, she cracked open the door to see a dark-haired, heavy man meander over to the television and turn it on. He then stretched, walked over and got a drink, and headed for the restroom. Carolyn shut the door and walked down the hall, deciding to return when Mr. Holland was finished.

About fifteen minutes later, she headed back to room 643. The door was slightly ajar and Mr. Holland's loud, demanding voice reverberated in the hallway. "How dare you ask me to move. Don't you know anything? What kind of a nurse are you anyway? I bet you don't even have a degree. I was in a car accident. Do I need to spell it for you? C-a-r a-c-c-i-d-e-n-t. I can't move anything. I can't walk—I'll probably be paralyzed for life. Bring me my blanket and my lunch. Now! Oh, and find someone to rub my feet."

Carolyn's ire rose faster than the twenty-something nurse bolted from the room. She pushed open the door and marched resolutely across the floor.

Mr. Holland's gaze met hers. "You got my lunch yet? It better be hot. You the one who's going to feed me? Or are you the foot rubber?"

"Mr. Holland. Not only am I not going to feed you, I'm not going to get you a blanket, and I wouldn't touch your feet with a ten-foot pole."

"Excuse me?" the red-faced Holland sputtered.

Carolyn's voice dropped. "I know your kind. I saw scores of them throughout my long career. You aren't really hurt, but you will milk this for all it's worth. You'll lie and twist the truth to get money from the insurance company and the other driver. You'll lie and fake your injuries to make the hospital staff kowtow to your every whim. You'll lie and try to justify having your family wait on you hand and foot. But when everyone's not looking, you'll stand up and walk yourself over to the TV, pour yourself a drink, use the restroom, and not have an ache or a pain."

Carolyn paused, then pointed to her nameplate. "Well, buddy, not me. This sign may say 'Volunteer,' but it certainly doesn't say 'stupid' or 'doormat.' You want your feet rubbed? I suggest you get a cat!"

Mr. Holland's face froze with shock. A myriad of emotions visibly played across his large features, as if his brain were broadcasting his thoughts aloud: "How does she know? Could she have seen me? Nah, she can't know. She must be guessing." Finally, he spoke. "I don't know what you're talking about. I'm in terrible pain. I may never walk again. Someone will hear about this. My lawyer will hear about this. The hospital will hear about this. If it's the last thing I do, I will make sure you regret your words to me for the rest of your life."

Carolyn stared at him stonily. "Mister, I can guarantee you that of my regrets in life, you will not even be on the list. If

I recall, the Scriptures say something about honesty and taking advantage of others. In the end, sir, if you do not change your ways and repent, I believe *you* might be the one with some eternal regrets. While you have all this spare time on bed rest due to your supposed injuries, you might want to think about that." With that her final declaration, Carolyn turned and marched out of his room.

Mr. Holland was true to his word. Before finishing her shift, Carolyn was informed she would no longer be welcome in Geriatrics but would be transferred to the Pediatric Unit. Riding home in the car, she railed, "Ruth, that man was crookeder than half the inmates at the county jail—and meaner than the other half. How could the hospital defend him?"

In classic Ruth style, her friend grabbed Carolyn's hand and responded, "Well, I for one couldn't care less what the hospital did. I think you have a heart of gold to defend that nurse the way you did and to put Mr. Holland in his place. I wish I had the courage to do it. I also thought it was admirable how you stood up and delivered that sermon."

"Sermon? That was a tirade, not a sermon."

"Carolyn, I know you don't often talk openly about God, but when you stood up and told that man he needed to repent, I bet our heavenly Father was right proud of what you did. I know I was."

Carolyn shrugged Ruth's comments off but couldn't help revisiting them later when she was alone, snuggled up on her couch. Gazing out her window at the salmon-tinged clouds unnaturally suspended in the pretwilight sky, she wondered: Did she really not talk about God very much—even to Ruth, her dearest friend? Why was that? She believed. It just seemed she really hadn't needed Him all that much. With her career and busy life, she hadn't had much time for recreation, men, or God. Now she had lost everything. Did she blame Him? Did she need Him? Did she have the right to ask Him for help now, after all the years of ignoring Him? Carolyn went to bed with far more questions than answers.

Tuesday dawned bright and provided a marked contrast to Carolyn's outlook for the day. "Volunteer shmolunteer," she muttered as she put the finishing touches on her hair. "Demoted from sixth floor to fifth in one day. At this rate I'll only have five more shifts before I'm out of there. If the hospital kicks me out, even Ruth will have to admit that her rose-colored glasses, when it comes to my charitable personality traits, have to go." The thought of escaping Ruth's guilt trips once and for all spurred Carolyn out the front door to her friend's waiting vehicle.

The drive to the hospital consisted of a crash course in caring for children. Despite visiting her niece Emily and her young charges, and periodic visits to Ruth's house as her children were growing, Carolyn was not what one would call child-friendly. She certainly had no experience handling kids alone.

"Now how do you fasten a diaper again? Are there instructions on it?" Carolyn asked, rapidly jotting notes while they talked.

"Carolyn, relax. You'll do fine. It's a diaper, not a bag of microwave popcorn. There are no instructions on the package. You just affix the tabs. Somebody there will show you what to do." Ruth shook her head at her friend's unaccustomed lack of expertise.

Diapers turned out to be the least of Carolyn's worries. Storytime was her assignment, and she was elated. "Reading a book—right up my alley." She picked up her reading material and thumbed through the pages. "Twenty-five pages—not bad. Looks like a short day for Volunteer Sheffield."

Her confidence was short-lived. Opening the door to a room of over twenty active preschoolers stopped her in her tracks. Fortunately, Nurse Jana was on hand. "They are so wiggly. And noisy. How do I get their attention?" Carolyn asked, stress evident in her voice.

"Piece of cake. I've got you covered. Go sit over there in that chair." Jana pointed to a seat in the middle of the throng of three-footers. As soon as Carolyn was seated, Jana placed her fingers in her mouth and blew a whistle louder than any Carolyn had ever heard.

Apparently Carolyn wasn't the only one surprised. A hush fell over the curious crowd, all frozen in midactivity.

Jana addressed her audience. "Boys and girls, please find your seats. Our special reader today will be Ms. Sheffield. She has a wonderful story to share with you."

At the invitation to find a seat, Carolyn found a mass of five young but vigorous bodies competing for her lap. The victor, a blond, pig-tailed girl, straightened her garments messed in the battle and wiggled to find a comfortable spot.

She turned, looked at Carolyn, and announced, "You do *not* have a gramma's lap. It's not comfy or soft like it's supposed to be."

Carolyn wasn't in the mood for criticism, especially from a three year old, but she let it lie. "That's because I'm not a gramma."

A chorus of "Why?" arose, leading unsuspecting Carolyn down a path trickier than any she had seen in her legal career. Each answer she provided was countered by another "Why?"

When, after a half hour, Nurse Jana poked her head back in the room, the book still lay on Carolyn's lap unopened, and she was exhausted, inextricably entangled in the *why* web of the three-year-olds' world.

"This audience was tougher than any group of defense counsel I've seen. I'm worn out," Carolyn later explained to Jana, after admitting the book hadn't even been opened. "I am a fish out of water when trying to deal with these small children. I think they can smell that I'm a rookie. Ruth's the grandmotherly type. I'm not even sure I'm the mother type, much less a grandmother figure." She stared at Jana with pleading eyes and produced the best lost-puppy look she could muster. "Please, please get me out of here. I'll do anything."

Within a week, Carolyn found out what her "anything" would be. When she showed up for her shift early the next Saturday morning, she was ushered into the Transitional Care Unit.

"This is a rather unusual case," Ethel, the volunteers coordinator, explained. "We are experimenting with increasing the personal contact our comatose patients are receiving, to see if it has an effect on their recovery rates. We're asking people to talk with them, hold their hands, and communicate with them as if they were fully aware. We're not exactly sure what effect it will have, but we know it can't hurt." Ethel paused outside a door marked TCU 121, 122, 123 and ran her fingers through her large gray curls.

"We would like to assign you to be the one-on-one caregiver for Marti Thule. She's seventeen years old. She was in a car accident four weeks ago and has been in a coma ever since. It will be a big commitment and will take a lot of time, so I want you to see Marti and think about it before you decide." Ethel met Carolyn's gaze. "If you accept this assignment, it will be important for you to follow through. She's behind the first partition. I'll be at the nurses' station if you need me."

Carolyn pushed open the white curtain surrounding bed 121. Lying on the pillow, the flesh color of her face starkly contrasting with the sea of white about her, was a petite, auburn-haired teen. "So young and with so much life left to live," Carolyn mused. The face reminded her a bit of Emily at a much younger age. As Carolyn gazed down at the helpless girl, an indescribable feeling came over her. She immediately headed out of the room and down to the nurses' station. She wasn't sure why, but Carolyn knew exactly what she was supposed to do. Carolyn Sheffield, Volunteer, had a new assignment.

fourteen

Seventy-one-year-old attorney and widower Michael Flannigan brushed a stray white lock away from his piercing blue eyes and stared at the five-two hurricane who was verbally assaulting him. Stunned from the attack, he speechlessly watched her spin on her heel and march across the dance floor. When he realized her irate dressing-down had brought the attention of the rest of his colleagues and friends, his silence turned to explanation. Not sure what had generated the rash of accusations, he joked with the very interested crowd, "Oh, apparently cousin Mary's forgotten to take her medication again. I'll have to get hold of her doctor."

A wave of laughter seemed to pacify their nosy curiosity but did nothing to quell Michael's own questions. Despite his lighthearted comment, this was not cousin Mary, and she was saner than any woman he'd seen in awhile. She was also angrier. Even after replaying the episode again and again in his head, Michael couldn't for the life of him figure out what he had done to set her off.

He returned to his spacious condominium overlooking Lake Union and headed for bed. After tossing and turning for forty minutes, Michael had to admit the futility of the exercise. Sleep was not coming. He went to the living room and leaned against the window, gazing at the reflection of the pumpkin moon in the purple-tinged water. A familiar thought crossed his mind, as it often did when he observed some of God's more glorious creations: *Are You finding as much pleasure in the beautiful work of Your hands as I am right now? Thank You. It is amazing.* The first thought was followed by a second, equally familiar: *Too bad Elise is not here to share it with me.*

Even absorbing the beauty of the night couldn't rid Michael's mind of the evening's events. What had he done to set the spitfire of a woman off? Why did he care so much? Michael was not one easily riled. In just fewer than fifty years of marriage to Elise, he could remember only a handful of occasions on which they had quarreled. Sweet Elise. How different she was from the little fireball who assailed him tonight. She *never* would have done anything like that. Tall and refined, she was more the "scrub the floor in silence" type when she was upset with him. Boy, he missed her. Even though it had been almost five years since he lost Elise, it seemed like she was with him constantly. No other woman had caught his attention or eye since. Until tonight. For some unexplainable reason, Michael felt drawn to the feisty woman who had whisked on and off the dance floor in a flurry of angry energy.

Staring at the stars dancing on the night waves, Michael wondered whether she would ever cross his path again. And if he'd ever find out what he, or whoever the cad she thought he was, had done to raise her ire.

Michael didn't have long to wait for an answer to his midnight reflections. Two-and-a-half weeks later, he headed to Community Memorial for some medical tests. After spending a good hour as a human pincushion, Michael emerged poked, pricked, and prodded.

"Doctors," he muttered. "What a job. They spend all day inflicting pain and discomfort, yet they are still revered and well paid. Maybe I should change professions."

His half-hearted comments were interrupted by a sweet voice calling his name.

"Michael Flannigan? Is that you?"

Michael turned to see the familiar white-haired owner of

the honey voice. "Ruth Welch. How are you? It's been so long since I have talked with you. I thought I'd run into you at the hospital fund-raiser, but you must have escaped before I could snag a dance. What brings you here today?"

"You know me. Every chance I get to volunteer here at Community, I take." Ruth turned her head and scanned the halls. "Wait here. There's someone I'd like you to meet." With a quick wave, the little woman hurried down the corridor.

Michael leaned against the wall and smiled. For Ruth Welch he'd do anything. The woman had a heart that rivaled Texas in size. When Ruth had heard of Elise's passing, she had provided him meals for a month. Often he'd come home to find a casserole on the porch and a "Made a little extra tonight" note attached. Any friend of that saintly woman had to be worth meeting. He closed his eyes and waited.

His reverie was interrupted by a familiar anger-tinged voice. "What are *you* doing here?"

He quickly opened his eyes to find a memorable glare affixed to the middle of his forehead. Looking past the steely glare, he met the gaze of a clearly perplexed Ruth.

"Carolyn? Have you met Michael?" Ruth asked.

"Met him? How soon you forget. I gave him the dressing-down of a lifetime. It was well-deserved, I might add." Carolyn's fixed stare dared Michael to move.

Ruth's love-lined face showed rare consternation. "I don't understand. Michael is my friend."

It was Carolyn's turn to look concerned. "Now I'm the confused one. I mean, forgive and forget is one thing, Ruth, but it's only been a couple of weeks since this cad humiliated you to tears. I know the Scriptures talk about turning the other cheek, but how can you deem him your friend?"

Ruth's face reddened until it matched Carolyn's coat. "*This* is the man you dressed-down? *This* is the man who received your wrath? Oh, Carolyn. This is my old friend Michael

Flannigan whom I told you about. Don't you remember? He wasn't the man who rejected me at the dance."

Michael watched as recognition, then remorse, passed through Carolyn's eyes.

Extending her hand, she took his and grumbled out an apology. "So sorry. Looks like I got the wrong man."

Even in the obvious throes of embarrassment, this woman was formidable.

"It's all right," Michael assured. "If I'd heard the man reject my dear Ruth, I would have had a word or two for him myself. Although," he added with a wink at the shuffling Carolyn, "I don't think I could have produced a performance to equal yours."

Ruth wasted no time taking advantage of the lull in the apology-fest. "Michael, have you had lunch? Carolyn and I were about to get something to eat and would love a hand-some male escort."

Michael knew better than to let that invitation pass him by. This was his chance to get to know a little about the woman who had occupied so much of his thoughts the last couple of weeks.

"You bet I'm in." He deviously smiled at Carolyn and added, "As long as your friend promises to treat me to dessert for the terrible way she spoke to me. We men have fragile egos, you know."

Carolyn snorted at his feigned hurt. "I worked with a bunch of male attorneys. You better try the fragile-ego line on someone other than this seasoned gal. I'm old enough to know better. Dessert, however, I will do."

The afternoon flew by as Michael and Carolyn parried with sarcasm under chaperone Ruth's watchful and obviously pleased eyes. Before parting, matchmaker Ruth invited Michael and Carolyn over to her house for dinner the next evening. Michael observed Carolyn's response very carefully.

"We'll see, Ruth. I'll have to get back with you about that when I have my schedule in front of me," Carolyn offered, her voice not giving Michael much hope she'd be anywhere near Ruth's house the following night.

When Ruth attempted to insist, Michael observed Carolyn's set jaw. *This woman is one to be reckoned with,* he wryly noted.

His afternoon with Carolyn served to raise many questions in his mind. She was highly intelligent. She was also fiercely loyal, as he had found out during their unfortunate first encounter. There was something else, however. She had a protective wall around her. Michael wondered if anyone had ever been able to penetrate it. What had put it there in the first place? Would she ever be willing to take it down?

Thoughts of Carolyn, along with the unanswered questions, accompanied him far into the night as Michael and the moon kept watch over Lake Union.

ଈ

Carolyn straightened the white silk collar on her button-down blouse and pulled on a tailored vest with her volunteer name badge affixed. Although she had only spent two afternoons with Marti Thule, she felt as if she knew the girl. Spending time with the young lady, poised on the brink of life's opportunities yet unable to take advantage of any of them, released a flood of Carolyn's own emotions. She fiddled for a few more seconds before the mirror, grabbed a bunch of radiant gerbera daisies in a vase, and headed for her much-anticipated visit with Marti.

When Carolyn arrived at the Transitional Care Unit, she went into Marti's room, placed the bright bouquet on her bedside table, and grabbed her hand. Speaking in hushed tones so as not to disturb the patron on the other side of the cloth divider, Carolyn addressed her new friend.

"Well, dear, I wish you could see the flowers, but let me tell you about them. Gerberas are my favorites, and these are glorious shades of jeweled purple, red, orange, and yellow. I had to go to a special florist to get them this time of year, but they are worth it. They bring an instant kaleidoscope of colored light to any room, even on the dreariest days. You know, I've never been a roses kind of gal. Funny thing is, not one of my would-be suitors over the last fifty or so years could tell you that. I guess none of them ever cared to know me well enough to ask. Have had more roses than I've ever cared to see, though. I'm sure there are a lot of folks at the local retirement home wondering where all those large rose bouquets came from."

Carolyn paused, still tightly gripping the girl's seemingly life-less, tube-punctured hand. Fifty years of painful memories overwhelmed her. Safe in this room with a captive, albeit silent, audience, Carolyn allowed the feelings she normally would have banished to the deepest crevice in her mind to surface. She softly continued, "You know it's not that I wouldn't have loved a fresh flower bouquet, or someone who cared enough to figure out what I liked. In fact, I thought I had found love once. I was a young thing—barely older than you." Carolyn looked down at the unlined face of youth on the pillow.

"A handsome fellow. Magazine-cover handsome. Smart to boot. I was new at the law firm. A bit of a thing, naive and young. He worked three floors above and swept me off my feet. Dinner invitations. Flowers. The works. He was a smooth cookie, and I fell like an anvil—hard. Couldn't pass him in the elevator without my heart pounding like I had just com-pleted the first half of the Boston Marathon. After a couple of dinners, I knew. He was the one. I couldn't believe God had found me such a great husband. The man gave me a ring and told me he wanted to marry me after six months. He asked me not to tell people at the firm about us, because there was a policy concerning colleagues becoming romanti-cally involved." Carolyn's voice faltered.

"Funny. Seems like yesterday in some respects. I went up to his office one day to drop off some lunch. His secretary took the bag. She then took my heart when she said, 'I'll deliver it as soon as his wife leaves.' I took off my ring, put it in the lunch bag, and left. Never told a soul. Didn't even talk to God about it. Too humiliated and ashamed. Wasn't sure exactly how to approach it with Him. 'Please heal my heart that the married man I was in love with broke,' somehow didn't sound too good, so I just let it lie." Carolyn stopped her reminiscing and let the wave of pent-up emotion keep her company. Much later, she placed a kiss on Marti's cheek and silently walked the hallway toward the neon green Exit sign.

Carolyn numbly drove home, feeling strangely peaceful, despite the exhausting emotional battle she had waged this afternoon. *What would God have done if I had turned it over to Him? Would He have condemned me for my stupidity and relationship with a married man?* In the back of her head, a still, small voice asked, *Or would He have taken you in His loving arms, knowing you hadn't known, and healed your broken heart?*

Pulling into her driveway, Carolyn dragged herself from her vehicle and up the front steps of her home. A heavy Seattle mist bathed her in gray. Even in her exhaustion, she couldn't miss the brown box on her doorstep. Lifting the lid, Carolyn found the largest bouquet of wildflowers she had ever seen. When she took them into the light of her house, Carolyn gasped. Amidst the other flowers, three dozen gerbera daisies stood tall.

For the first time in as long as Carolyn Sheffield could remember, she allowed herself to cry.

fifteen

Carolyn's musings of the last week finally found a voice. "Three dozen gerberas, Marti. Can you believe it? Who could have sent them?"

As usual, her silent companion provided no answer. "You know," Carolyn's voice added in the silence, "I haven't even told Ruth about receiving them. With that ammunition she'd have me hooked, tied, and down the aisle with any one of her 'dashing and highly eligible' senior gentlemen before I could stop it. At least for now, I have to play this one close to the vest. I can't imagine any man who knows me well enough to know my weakness for those daisies. For that matter, I can't imagine any man who would make the effort and go to the expense of finding them this time of year!"

Carolyn sat quietly in the room, her mind running through the possibilities. Finally, her growling stomach broke her train of thought. She squeezed Marti's hand. "Well, dear. My stomach is calling. I'll be back in a few minutes, after I grab a bite to eat."

Carolyn shut the door to bed 121 and set off to find Ruth. *Wonder if she can break for lunch?* When she finally tracked Ruth down, her friend's hurried gait, pink cheeks, and harried smile answered Carolyn's question. Pediatrics, Ruth's work assignment this week, was hopping today. Carolyn would be dining alone.

She aimed her now starving body toward the cafeteria in search of lunch. Halfway down the hall, a vaguely familiar voice heralded her. "Carolyn?"

Turning abruptly, Carolyn was surprised to see the still

dashingly handsome owner of the voice. Unwilling to let Michael believe she remembered his name, Carolyn smiled. "Fred, how have you been?"

Michael's slightly furrowed brow spoke louder than words. Carolyn wasn't sure whether this man bought that she was suffering from memory loss. His consternation turned to a large grin.

"You know, only my more formal acquaintances call me Fred. Close friends call me Michael. I know we'll become close friends, so please feel free to call me Michael. Let's go grab a bite to eat."

Carolyn, for once, was speechless. This man not only ignored her deliberate indifference but also had the courage to insist they'd become close friends and ask her to lunch. She didn't quite know what to make of him or the weird fluttering feeling she had in her stomach each time she saw him. *It's those dashing good looks,* she tried to convince herself. *If he were an average Joe, I'd have him wrapped, packaged, and sent on his way without a second thought.* But even as the words played through her head, they didn't quite ring true.

Suddenly realizing her thoughts had left her standing speechless in front of this man who was, with obvious enjoyment, awaiting her answer, Carolyn cleared her throat. "I'm on my way down to the cafeteria if you'd like to join me— Fred." She walked resolutely down the hall, not even pausing to see if he were following.

As she rounded the corner to the lunch line, Michael's much larger stride enabled him to catch up with her shorter but quick-paced stride. A bit out of breath, he joked, "I hope my wallet will hold out. The way you charged to the cafeteria, you must be hungry enough to eat an elephant."

Carolyn had to smile. Her efforts to ditch Michael seemed to not be working. Despite her apparent failure to shake him, Carolyn wasn't upset. In fact, she felt rather exhilarated.

Maybe this fellow wasn't so bad after all. Not that she'd ever tell him, but deep down, Carolyn found herself enjoying the encounter.

Plate piled high, Carolyn headed for the register. She was hungry. If Michael wanted to foot the bill, he'd find out just *how* hungry. When she slid her tray next to his, he didn't even blink. "I love a woman with an appetite. I'm so glad you feel comfortable enough in my company to eat. I can't stand it when a woman picks around a plate trying to convince you she eats like a bird, and goes home hungry. Senseless."

Carolyn had said the same thing to Ruth many times but wasn't about to admit to Michael that she saw eye to eye with him on this, or anything else. "Hmm," was her non-committal reply.

Carolyn had as much fun at lunch as she'd had in a long time. Long-dammed-up laughter escaped in uncontrollable bursts. Carolyn knew her best efforts couldn't hide the fact that she was having a marvelous time with her luncheon companion. She went to grab another soft drink and tried to get her schoolgirl enthusiasm under control. When she returned to the table, a second man was standing there.

Michael rose to his feet and introduced Carolyn. "Bob Marin. Carolyn Sheffield. Bob is one of my oldest friends. Carolyn. . ."—Michael turned with a deliberate wink in Bob's direction—"is one of my newest friends."

"Sheffield." Bob rubbed his hand over his hair-challenged scalp. "Do you come from the Boston Sheffields?"

Carolyn responded. "Oh, no. Not the Boston Sheffields. Didn't even know there were any. I'm from the much more auspicious Alderdale Sheffield clan."

"Alderdale?" Bob's furrow met his long, receding hairline. "Alderdale, Oregon?"

"That's the one," Carolyn proudly replied.

"One of my dearest friends lives in Alderdale. Absolute

gem of a woman. Perhaps you know her." Bob shook his head as if he couldn't believe his faux pas. "What am I thinking? Of course you must know her. If that saint and gentlewoman resides in the town, her good works and fingerprints have made their way all over it. Alderdale—lucky home of Harriet Taylor."

The mention of Harriet's name with the glowing endorsement was too much for Carolyn. The drink she had so demurely sipped during his oration on Alderdale flew across the table, propelled by her shock. When it sprinkled Michael's plate like spring rain, his response set off her jangled nerves.

"Just what I needed. My food was a little dry." Michael winked and continued to eat his soft-drink speckled entree.

Carolyn erupted in gales of uncontrolled laughter. Tears coursed down her cheeks unheeded. Embarrassment at totally losing control in front of the two men did nothing to stop her. When she finally calmed down, she managed to say between remaining chuckles, "Harriet's fingerprints *are* all over the town, that's for sure. Her footprints are there, too." She left out the fact that the footprints were all over the backs of those Harriet had walked on.

Bob stared at Carolyn like she was an absolute loon, but Michael's face was tinged with obvious amusement. The men said their good-byes. Yet even after Bob left the table, he continued to look over his shoulder as if he had severe questions regarding her sanity.

Carolyn resumed finishing her drink. She had been so amused by the image Bob had painted of her meddling cousin, she had overlooked a very disturbing possibility. Could Bob's involvement with Harriet and Michael be just coincidence? If Carolyn had learned anything over the years it was that "coincidence" and "Harriet Taylor" didn't normally fall in the same sentence. Carolyn's defense system, so recently let down, was instantly reactivated. Could this be one of Harriet's matchmaking ruses? As much as she didn't want to believe it, she couldn't dismiss the idea outright. She'd have to watch this fellow.

"Well, Fred, it's been fun, but I have to head back to my volunteer duties. See you around." Carolyn stood with her drink, and her new set of disturbing questions, and prepared to make a quick exit.

Michael rose to bid her farewell, confusion written all over his rugged face.

Carolyn headed to her car before returning to Marti's room armed with a sack. After bringing the girl up to date on the lunchroom dramatics, Carolyn reached into the bag and brought out a leather-bound journal. "I was going through some old boxes in my garage the other day and found this book." She opened the pages gingerly and turned to a black-and-white picture of a teenage girl.

"I knew you reminded me of my niece, Emily, but until I found this picture, I didn't realize how much you resembled her. It's amazing. You know, life dealt her some major blows, just like you. She thought she'd never be able to fulfill some of her dreams, but she held on. She found love and happiness, and just last spring, she was married at the ripe old age of forty-six. Marti, what I'm trying to say is, even though things look rough from where you are right now, hang on. God has a plan for you. I'm not sure what it is, but I promise: He does. Just like He had a plan for Emily." *And,* added a small voice in her head, *like He still has a plan for you, Carolyn Sheffield.*

Carolyn read from her journal the remainder of the afternoon. Visions of a much younger and much more vulnerable woman filled the corners of the room. Stories of rejection, pain, and heartache touched the mature woman who now remembered the events with a much more analytical eye. Editorial comments interspersed her reading. "Should have known better on that one." "Look, girl, can't you see him coming from a mile away?" "Good riddance to the cad."

Carolyn was surprised to find some prayer entries in her journal; the heartfelt petitions she had written to her heavenly Father she could now see had been answered. Some had taken years, but the benefit of time's passage now opened the much older woman's eyes. At what point had she stopped journaling? At what juncture had she decided she didn't have time to pray? Looking back through the journal pages, it was clear those decisions had been made long before the Lord answered many of her prayers.

"So," she quietly reflected, "even though I gave up on Him, He never gave up on me. He continued to answer my prayers from long ago, even when I no longer asked. He remembered." For the second time in as many weeks, tears followed the lines of Carolyn's face.

"Oh, bother. If I keep this up, it's going to become a habit," she muttered, wiping the stray droplets from her cheeks. "Good thing no one is around. They'd think I was a dotty old woman." Even for all her bluster, Carolyn Sheffield knew today was a day that would change her life.

After kissing her friend Marti on the forehead, Carolyn left the hospital. Instead of heading for home, she drove to West Seattle. She parked at Lincoln Park and headed across the grassy lawn. Peeling madrona trees beautifully framed Puget Sound's angry gray waves below. The blustery wind on the beach walk pushed at Carolyn's small body, daring her to try to walk. She tucked her head against the wind's power and propelled her body forward, despite the powerful gusts. Out in nature, battling the elements, Carolyn felt renewed. The spray of salty water carried on the wind stung her face but awakened her senses.

Though the inclement weather had chased off much of the human population, Carolyn braved the elements and found strength. Standing on a piling, she held up her arms and shouted, "I, Carolyn Sheffield, am alive!" Her words were swallowed by the hungry wind as soon as they were uttered. The almost-seventy-year-old woman continued, shouting into the wind, "I am sorry. Please forgive me."

The wind screamed louder.

"I'm sorry I forgot You. I love You. Please don't leave me!" The answering howl of the wind knocked Carolyn from her weathered piling. Sitting on the rocky, wet ground, she quietly added, "I can't do it without You."

As soon as the words left her lips, an unnatural calm fell over the beach. The wind's gyrations quelled. The leftover breezes skimmed waves and left them dancing. Peace filled Carolyn from head to toe. She felt as if warm, loving arms had encircled her in an embrace. The warmth had a familiar feel.

Carolyn stayed on the beach until the last rays of the brilliant sunset dimmed, then disappeared. Even after the sun's rays were gone, she did not feel the winter chill of the night air. The continued warmth of a heavenly embrace reminded Carolyn Sheffield that she had returned home.

sixteen

"If I find out Harriet Taylor has stuck her meddling paws into my pot of honey, that woman will rue the day she was born," Carolyn threatened over the phone.

Her softer niece, Emily Carr Hamilton, replied in kind. "I know. I'm very familiar with those 'paws.' Remember, I was her 'cause of the month' for awhile."

"Emily, I really am relying on you. Track her. Spy on her. Follow her. Whatever you need to do. Just find out whether she has anything to do with sending a Mr. Michael Flannigan my way." Carolyn's normal control wavered slightly. "It's really important." After a pause, she added. "Of course, if that woman is involved, I'm sure it won't take much undercover work to find it out. She'll be announcing her 'charitable efforts' on my behalf all over Alderdale."

Emily assured Carolyn she would search out the truth. "Just tell me: Is he as bad as Herman Dobbs? I knew *I* couldn't control Harriet, but I thought for sure she'd leave *you* alone. I mean, you're so—formidable."

"If she is involved, Harriet will find out firsthand how formidable I can be. And no, I wouldn't say this fellow is of the Herman Dobbs ilk."

Carolyn gathered from Emily's silence that she knew better than to press the Michael Flannigan issue.

Carolyn found comfort in the knowledge she would soon have the answers to the questions that had plagued her since her meeting three weeks earlier with Michael and his staunch Harriet-supporting friend, Bob Marin. She sat down in her plush living room, armed with a grapefruit and a spoon, and contemplated the events of the last month.

The intensity of the turmoil she felt over the possibility that her relationship with Michael was of Harriet's making, surprised her. Either she was becoming soft in her old age or the fellow had worked his way under her shell far more effectively than she had believed. She had tried to peg the strong feelings in the "overflow from her deeply spiritual experience" column but knew instinctively that they didn't fit there. Funny, she was awaiting Emily's return call almost as much as a teenager awaits a call asking her out on a prom date. The fluttery feelings were back in her stomach, too.

The ringing of her doorbell interrupted Carolyn's contemplation. She grabbed a sweater and went to answer it. When she reached the front door, the disappearing UPS delivery truck caused her to glance down. A medium-sized package lay on her porch. *I didn't order anything,* Carolyn thought as she scanned the box for a nonexistent return address. Shutting the door and opening the box, Carolyn was shocked to see a beautiful, brand-new leather-bound journal. She was also amazed by the pound of See's chocolates, her absolute favorite. Her disbelief continued when, upon opening the box, she discovered that whoever ordered them knew her far better than she thought anyone did. Inside was a full pound of orange creams. No one, besides Ruth, knew of Carolyn's addiction to the orange-filled rounds of light chocolate. Her monthly trek to downtown Seattle to pick up a small stash was top secret.

"Who on earth?" Carolyn muttered aloud.

Later that night, Carolyn posed the same question, but to a higher source. "Heavenly Father, You obviously know who is doing this. I trust You. Please, just don't let me get hurt." Although she didn't receive an answer telling her who was delivering the gifts, Carolyn once again felt at peace.

A week later, armed with her new journal, Carolyn headed toward the hospital for a much-anticipated meeting with

Marti. She couldn't wait to tell the girl her exciting news. It appeared that Michael Flannigan had been exonerated. Emily's call indicated Harriet hadn't seemed to know anything about Michael, although mention of his friend Bob had sent Harriet into a lengthy adoration-fest. According to Emily, no mention of Harriet's "good deeds" or Carolyn Sheffield had made their way around the Alderdale rumor circuit, either.

When Carolyn passed the hospital desk on her way to her friend's room, the now-familiar ladies at the nurses' station greeted her. "How are you doing this morning, Carolyn? What did you bring for Marti today?"

The peppery charge nurse, Denise, brushed her short gray hair behind her ear, and came around the desk. "I'll tell you, I don't care what the study says, I can attest that your visits with Marti have done wonders. Even though she hasn't come out of the coma, there is a peace about her that has developed in the months you have worked with her." She gave Carolyn a hug. "Thank you so much for spending so much time with her. You have been a godsend."

Carolyn nodded. If Denise only knew. God *had* sent her to Marti; she was sure of that. But Carolyn didn't think it was only for Marti's benefit. The blessings had been Carolyn's.

Working her way down the hall, Carolyn stopped when she heard voices emerging from Marti's room. The muffled conversation took shape as she drew closer to the slightly ajar door.

Dr. Duncan's recognizable voice drifted into the hall. "I can't give you any guarantees. We're not even sure how much brain activity is there. Sometimes miracles happen, even after months and months. I really don't know whether this will be one of those. It has to be your decision, though."

"I wish Mom and Dad were still alive," a young female voice lamented. "They'd know what to do for Marti."

A male voice piped in. "They aren't. As her brother and

sister, we have to make a choice. Marti was full of life. You know that. She would have hated to see herself this way. She's not going to get better. There has been plenty of time for a miracle. You heard what Dr. Duncan said—she could stay on life-support for years and years and never come out of it. I say we disconnect her and let her go. She was always a free spirit. I say we let her fly."

The sister's voice acquiesced with relief that someone else was making the decision. "If you really think it's best. . . Anyway, she'll be with Mom and Dad."

Carolyn could hold back no longer. Bursting into the room, she addressed the shocked young people in front of her. "Miracles do happen. Sometimes it takes a lot longer than we think, but if there's any chance at all, don't you think Marti deserves to have that chance?" Carolyn's severe demeanor dissolved as she pleaded. "She's my friend. I know she's getting better. Even the nurses here see it. Ask them. Please. Let me work with her for a little longer. Let me have a little more time. I'll come every day. Please, just don't give up on her yet."

The brother's obviously harried face grew stern. "Who is this woman?" he asked a shocked-looking Dr. Jensen. He turned his wrath on Carolyn. "What do *you* know? You didn't live with her for almost twenty years. You didn't grow up with her. You didn't comfort her when our parents died. She's not *your* younger sister. She's ours. She was in a coma months ago. She is in a coma now. Time isn't going to change that. I suggest you attend to your own affairs." The man's veins bulged in anger. "And stay out of our business."

Realizing what she had done, Carolyn fled from the room and out of the hospital. Tears coursed down her cheeks with the realization that her dear friend Marti would not be on this earth for much longer. Carolyn locked herself in her home, unplugged the phones, and refused to answer the door. Pain coursed through her body and doubled her in half. She wondered if she'd ever be able to breathe again as sob after sob shook her body.

Around four in the morning, Carolyn realized she had to go back to the hospital. If she only had a little time left with Marti, she didn't want to waste a moment. She gathered a few belongings and headed back to the Transitional Care Unit. When she stepped into the night air, it robbed her of breath and flash froze her lungs. She wrapped her coat close and braved the late winter night's fury.

As she passed the hospital desk, Denise's familiar, but utterly weary, face greeted her. "Carolyn. I held over on the night shift hoping you might come back. I wanted to talk with you. The administration found out what happened this afternoon. They have officially removed you from your duties."

The pain in Carolyn's solar plexus intensified. "What do you mean? I can't visit Marti anymore?"

The lines in Denise's face showed deep emotion, and she nodded. "That's exactly what it means." She took Carolyn's hand and led her down the hall toward the room. "I'm not supposed to do this, and it might cost me my job if they find out, but say your good-byes. At five A.M., no administrator I know is going to have a clue."

Carolyn slowly opened the door leading to bed 121. The familiar rhythm of the machines was missing. Marti lay on the pillow, unhooked from tubes and needles. Carolyn resumed her place at Marti's side, grasped the girl's hand, and squeezed out, past the lump in her throat, "Well, my dear, it looks like this is the end of the road for us. I'm sure glad I got a chance to meet you. I can't tell you what you have done for me. You know, this wasn't a real easy time in either of our lives. You got me through my tough time. I just wish I could have returned the favor."

Glancing down, tears formed in Carolyn's eyes. "I can give you one thing. The place you're going—well, I've got a contact up there. I'm sure He'll take real good care of you. I'll tell Him you are coming, and I'll ask Him to keep a special watch out for you. He'll make sure you feel at home. I promise."

Carolyn laid her old journal by Marti's bedside. "I would like you to have this. Because of you, I don't need the book to remember who I was and *whose* I was." Carolyn pointed to her head and then her heart. "You see, now I remember. Here and here."

Leaving her beloved journal at Marti's bedside, Carolyn squeezed her hand, planted one last kiss on her forehead, and choked out, "Good-bye."

❧

Carolyn flipped over in bed, attempting to ignore the incessant ringing of the doorbell. *Go away. Can't a person get some sleep?* The turning of a key in her front door lock let her know it was Ruth. *That will teach me to give her a spare key to my house,* Carolyn grumbled. The sound of small footsteps marched up the stairs toward Carolyn's room. Ruth's bright smile poked around the corner.

"There you are. Up and at 'em." Ruth attempted to help her friend rise.

"I'm tired. I'm staying in bed," Carolyn growled back.

"Oh, no, you don't, Ms. Grumpy. No healthy person needs a week in bed. Let's get you a nutritious breakfast."

"I'm not hungry, Ruth." Carolyn toned down her anger-filled voice. "I'm sorry. I'm not trying to be a bear. But I really don't feel like eating. Please, I just need a little space."

"If this is about you losing your volunteer position, I'm sure I can get you another one. You did a great job with that girl." Ruth's smile reminded Carolyn of a puppy dog's wagging tail, the animal just begging for a positive response.

Unfortunately, Carolyn was running a little short in the positive response department. "You don't understand. I don't want another volunteer position. I don't think I ever want to go back to the hospital."

The confusion broadcast across Ruth's caring face clearly showed she didn't fully understand why Marti meant so much to Carolyn, but Carolyn was not up to a heart-to-heart explanation, even for Ruth.

After a half hour of futile cajoling, Ruth worriedly left her friend, vowing to return soon. Less than an hour later, the doorbell rang again.

"When she said soon, she meant *soon,*" Carolyn mumbled. "Can't she take a hint?" Pulling herself out of bed in the hope that her friend might see her upright position as a sign she could leave, Carolyn went to answer the door.

When the door opened, Carolyn wished she were still snugly tucked underneath her covers. It was not Ruth who had come calling. It was a very dapper-looking Michael Flannigan.

Carolyn's hands went instinctively to the hairstyle her pillow had so painstakingly worked to create over the last three days. "Michael. So glad you could call. Do you always surprise your friends at the door, or do some warrant an advance phone call?" Carolyn's sarcasm was spurred by her embarrassment.

Michael appeared to ignore any unloving tone in Carolyn's voice. "I'm so glad you feel comfortable enough to call me by my real name. It's nice to know I've graduated from Fred to Michael."

Only after Michael mentioned it did Carolyn realize her slip. Not that it caused her much consternation. She was far more concerned about her sloppy attire and hairdo. Concentrating on the quickest way to the shower, Carolyn didn't object when Michael suggested that he walk around the block a couple of times while she got ready to go for a drive with him.

The cold pellets in the shower pierced the clouded thoughts that had kept Carolyn company since Marti's departure. Curiosity replaced numbness. Why did Michael want her to go for a ride with him? Where were they going?

It wasn't until hours later that Carolyn got her answers. Standing on a craggy rock high above Deception Pass, Michael finally broke the silence that the two had shared the entire drive up. "This is where I came when my wife, Elise, died. I thought you might find peace here, too."

Carolyn stared down the ragged, jutting slope. Waves sprayed the stark gray rocks as they passed through the narrow pass. Moss clung to the stone, as if daring to live and grow in an impossible environment. Caught in the harsh beauty of the place, Carolyn didn't even realize Michael had gone. How had he known this place would bring her comfort? How had he known she was in *need* of comfort? Carolyn forced her mind back into contemplating her natural surroundings. Today was a day for healing. The questions would wait for another day.

seventeen

The trip home from Deception Pass was much livelier than the wordless trek up. Although still grieving for the loss of her friend, out in the raw elements of God's creation, Carolyn had found a surprising salve for her pain. She could relate to the exposed rocks, constantly battered by the powerful waves. In a way, their constancy, challenging whatever the churning waters had to bring, empowered her. Life's blows of late had been harsh ones: the loss of her career and life's ambition; her confidence and will to continue; and her dear friend Marti.

Yet even though she felt the pain of the last months, a small voice reminded her that it had also been a time for gains: a rekindled relationship with her heavenly Father; Michael; and of course, sharing her life with Marti.

While Michael and she gently bantered in the car, Carolyn couldn't help but feel a small ray of hope pierce the dark shroud that encircled her. Michael turned the car into a parking lot and brought it to rest at the base of a fifteen-foot-tall ice cream cone. There wasn't much question what they were doing there. Carolyn couldn't remember the last time she had desired a late March ice cream. Hot chocolate, maybe, but not ice cream. Funny, after the odd day they had shared, ice cream seemed perfectly fitting.

Armed with treats in hand, Michael led Carolyn down a small dirt path that snaked around behind the hand-dipped ice cream place. Fifty yards down the path was a two-person wooden bench. The remnants of the tree trunk next to it hinted of its yesteryear grandeur. Crocus poked small bright heads up and surveyed the land.

Once they were seated, Michael said, "Why don't you tell me something about yourself that I don't know?"

Carolyn mentally noted that, given her reserve of late, it might be a very long list. She responded, "I worked as a paralegal downtown for almost fifty years. Seems like I was there every spare minute of my life, slaving away for the attorneys. Went in early. Came home late. Let's just say I was offered a retirement package that I really couldn't refuse."

"A really great one, huh?" Michael questioned.

"No. One I *really* couldn't refuse."

Michael's answering wince showed that he knew exactly what she was saying.

"I'll tell you, though," Carolyn continued, "I've had a lot of time in the last year to develop a great repertoire of attorney jokes. You want an attorney taken out at the knees, I'm your woman."

Carolyn wasn't sure how to read Michael's second wince.

Their bench conversation continued well into the early evening. Carolyn regaled Michael with stories of her early Alderdale escapades. Michael returned the favor by inviting her into the escapades of his younger years. Laughing, the two headed for the car. Michael opened Carolyn's door, then paused. "Thank you, Carolyn Sheffield, for letting me get to know you a little bit better." He winked, then added, "I don't care what all those other folks say. Deep down, you're a pretty good cookie."

Pleased, but slightly embarrassed by Michael's comment, Carolyn quipped, "You're not a bad egg yourself." When Michael walked around the car, Carolyn softly added, "And you'll never know how much today has meant to me."

After her excessive sleep of late, the next morning, Carolyn rose with the sun. She fiddled around the house, tackling chores that had been recently neglected. She showered, dressed, and readied herself for an early morning walk. Chaotic noise in her front yard sparked her curiosity. "What in the world is going on?" she muttered, making her way downstairs.

When she opened the door, it was all she could do not to slam it again. Standing in her doorway, casting a long shadow in the early morning sunshine, was Mr. Herman Dobbs, hat in hand and all five of his children in tow.

Carolyn gathered every ounce of politeness she could muster. "Why, Mr. Dobbs, what are *you* doing here?"

Herman's reply caught her completely off-guard.

"Well, Ms. Sheffield." He shifted his hat in his hands. "See, ever since my poor wife took ill and left me and the children, it's been awfully lonely 'round our house. I can't cook a lick. And as you know, my kids need someone to care for them. A mother figure. Ms. Taylor was mentioning your singleness and how you might be looking for a man. Since I'm looking for a woman, she—I mean I—thought you might be interested in being the woman in my home. You know, getting hitched and all."

Carolyn's laughter was tinged with compassion. "Herman Dobbs, I'm old enough to be a grandmother to your children. I may even be old enough to be a grandmother to you." The nods of the motley group assembled in her front yard indicated that she wasn't the only one who felt that way.

Carolyn's amusement still tickled the corners of her mouth. "Herman, have you ever thought of enrolling in a cooking school? They have plenty of great classes at local community colleges and community centers. I'm sure they even have one in Alderdale. Seems to me that if you took all the time Harriet has you running around on these wild goose chases and spent it in a cooking class, your problem might be solved."

A glimmer of thought showed on Herman's face. "They have classes like that?"

His interest provided Carolyn hope that maybe she was getting through to the man. "You better believe they do. I think you would do great there."

The hope brought by Herman's answering nod disappeared when he opined, "I bet there are a lot of ladies there who will be right good cooks when they're finished. Maybe I can find my wife there."

"Maybe, Herman." Carolyn shook her head. "Maybe."

The encounter left Carolyn in gales of laughter all morning long. Herman's visit, coupled with Emily's report that Harriet didn't have anything to do with Michael, settled her doubts once and for all. Michael was definitely a man of his own making.

"Now what am I going to do today to keep myself busy?" Carolyn contemplated. Today was her former volunteer day at the hospital. Even though Michael's companionship was filling some of the void left by Marti's departure, twinges of pain still haunted her. "I guess it's just a matter of time," she said. She combed her hair, threw on a light coat, and headed out to enjoy the sunshine. "Pain or not," Carolyn Sheffield vowed, "I'm going to live my life."

邊

If Michael Flannigan had thought Carolyn Sheffield was special at their initial meeting, he was hog-tied now. As much as he admired the woman's fire and indomitable spirit, he was equally, if not more, impressed by her tenderness and vulnerability. Not that she'd ever willingly let anyone see it, but circumstances had placed Michael in a position that he was able to see things he doubted many, if any, had seen before. Unfortunately, it seemed that as his love for her grew, the obstacles grew as well.

Why did it have to be a group of attorneys that had stung her? Why couldn't she have worked in a doctor's office or in a beauty shop? The thought of Carolyn in a beauty shop sent

Michael into a fit of laughter. "With her forthrightness, I can just see the havoc she'd wreak with beauty shop clientele. I don't suppose she'd have much use for the gossip and minutia, and I somehow don't see her holding her tongue."

Even with his temporary amusing reprieve, Michael still worried. How was he going to break it to this woman that he was of the same stripe as those who had ripped her life's rug out from underneath her? Right now, the last thing Michael Flannigan wanted to be was an attorney.

The questions plagued him the remainder of his exhausting day. He had to tell Carolyn. The longer he waited, the more she'd believe he was trying to deceive her. He knew he was in for a tongue-lashing regardless. It was not the lashing he was concerned about, though; he just didn't want to lose her. Given the upheaval in her life lately, would this be the last straw?

Even the thought of that outcome made him shudder. After discovering Carolyn, he wasn't about to let her get away. What should he do? Late into the evening, he pondered the question. Finally, he knelt down beside his bed.

"Well, Father, You know I never thought I'd find anyone after Elise. She was my love and my life. I was so blessed to have her and wouldn't change my life with her for anything. But now, You've brought this new woman into my life. Her energy and spirit renew me. She makes me glory in each day. I can't imagine spending the rest of my life without her. I think of her each waking moment. Help me. It seems as if forces are conspiring to keep us apart. Guide me that I might know what to say. Help me to find a way to get through to her. Bless me as I try to find ways to communicate my love to her. And be with me, Lord, that I may have more time on this earth to spend with Carolyn Sheffield."

Michael concluded his prayer and peacefully headed to bed. He wasn't sure what the solution would be, but long experience told him that whatever the outcome, the problem was now in the right place. He knew his heavenly Father would have the solution.

eighteen

Ruth anxiously perched on the edge of her chair in Carolyn's tastefully arranged living room, awaiting the next far-from-sordid detail in the Carolyn Sheffield/Michael Flannigan saga. Pleasure resonated from her face. "He drove you to Deception Pass? You had ice cream? If that doesn't beat all. If I didn't know better, Carolyn, I'd say you had yourself a suitor. I can't believe you didn't tell me sooner!"

Carolyn shrugged, trying to mask the excitement that she felt. "Oh, Ruth, we're just friends. I'm sure he just felt sorry for me."

Ruth's snort spoke loudly. She obviously wasn't buying that line. "Well, if I were you, I'd make sure to hold on to this one. I thought he was totally unavailable. After Elise, I assumed there would be no other woman in his life. Mark my words. Had I known, Michael Flannigan would have been number one on my list of potential dates. He's a keeper. Though what he sees in you, 'Ms. Hard-to-Get,' is beyond me. If you let him go, be warned. I'm next in line."

Ruth's wink and forthrightness made Carolyn laugh. Joined by her friend's chuckles, Carolyn warily admitted, "Amazingly enough, he *is* kind of getting to me. I'm not quite sure why. At first I thought it was his good looks. On appearance alone, that man would attract the attention of most women. It isn't that, though. I really am starting to like him. A lot."

Ruth's "I knew it" look, coupled with the shock her face reflected at hearing Carolyn admit it, started Carolyn's chuckles afresh. "Yes, Ruth. Me. Carolyn Sheffield, virtually seventy years old, smitten. I know. You don't have to say it. You never thought you'd see the day."

She stood and made her way to the kitchen with their empty lemonade glasses. As she turned the corner, she barely heard her friend's, "No, but I've always hoped and prayed I would."

❧

Carolyn found her admiration of Michael growing daily. Slowly, the all-consuming pain from losing Marti was replaced by anticipation of what the next day with Michael would hold. They trekked across the Northwest together, basking in the warm summer sun and observing the wonders of nature. Car rides were filled with laughter and poignant conversation about life and deity. Slowly, the woman who Carolyn had spent so much time concealing over the years, began to emerge.

Carolyn's seventieth birthday was spent with Michael, far from the reaches of Ruth's "likely to throw a surprise party" grasp. Michael picked her up early. After a long day's hike through the hills surrounding Leavenworth, Washington, Carolyn and Michael found a bit of needed shade under the lacy green leaves of a towering maple. "Boy, this is the life," Michael contentedly murmured.

"You said it," Carolyn responded. She took one of Michael's hands. "If I forget to tell you, thank you. The last few weeks have been wonderful, and even though I wasn't looking forward to the Big Seven-O, this has been one of the best birthdays I can remember. You really are a great guy."

Carolyn's unaccustomed journey into the sentimental seemed to startle Michael. He composed himself quickly. "You really deserve a great guy, but hold off on the compliments until you hear what I have to say."

Carolyn braced herself. This did not sound good.

Michael continued, his gaze fixed on the ground. "I've

wanted to tell you for awhile; I just didn't want to risk losing the relationship we have developed." He took her hand. "Carolyn, I am head over heels for you. When I leave you at night, I think about you. When I rise in the morning, you are the first thing that pops into my mind. I didn't think I'd ever feel this way about another woman. You are as different from my Elise as night is from the day, but my feelings toward you are equally strong."

Carolyn's pleasure over hearing his feelings for her was tempered by her concern over what his bad news would be. "Michael," she softly interrupted, "just get to the unpleasant part. Remember, 'Forward and Direct' is my motto."

Michael looked at her. "I never meant to deceive you. I didn't even know until a few weeks ago what your career circumstances had been. You once told me you could take any attorney out at the knees; I'm just hoping you'll spare mine."

She shook her head in confusion. "I don't understand. What are you saying?"

"Carolyn, I'm an attorney. Lawyer. Counselor at law. A J.D. Whatever you want to call it. Right now, I wish I was anything else. I know we're not your favorite breed on the planet. I think what happened to you was awful, and I'm truly sorry."

The shock of the news silenced Carolyn. This man, Michael Flannigan, was an attorney? It couldn't be. Betrayal and hurt filled every pore in Carolyn's body. Looking at Michael—his eyes tightly shut, obviously braced for one of Carolyn's infamous tongue-lashings—Carolyn couldn't oblige. The words caught in her throat. Why hadn't he told her? How long had he meant to deceive her? For the first time that day, Carolyn felt all of her seventy years.

She couldn't bear to look up again when she quietly said, "Please take me home."

The pleasant intermittent silence that had kept them

company on the drive over the mountains was replaced by an uncomfortable, brooding silence. Carolyn gazed stoically at the heat-scorched deciduous leaves. Their wilting appearance matched her mood. When Michael finally reached Carolyn's home, he went around and opened her car door. He awkwardly followed two paces behind her up to the front porch. "I'm sorry, Carolyn. I'm truly sorry. I should have told you earlier."

Carolyn said nothing. She marched inside and shut the door. Once on the other side of the closed front door, Carolyn allowed herself to feel the impact of what she had learned.

The doorbell interrupted her grief. Tempted to not answer it, Carolyn thought better of it and moved toward the door. Peeping through the hole, Carolyn was shocked to see her niece Emily. What was *she* doing here?

She didn't have to wait long to find out. After exchanging hugs and greetings, Emily exclaimed, "Happy birthday from Michael."

"Michael?" Even the sound of his name started the painful twinges. "What does he have to do with you?"

"He called me a month ago. He said he wanted to do something special for you for your birthday, and he thought you'd really enjoy a visit from me. He sent the plane ticket and arranged everything. I'm here for a week."

Carolyn was stunned. Michael had planned for Emily to come visit?

Emily continued, "I'll tell you, Aunt Carolyn, I don't know what Michael is like in person, but if his phone demeanor is even close to accurate, he is a wonderful man. And he is obviously very fond of you. How do you feel about him?"

Michael's recent confession, coupled with Emily's unanticipated question, was too much for Carolyn. The usually stoic aunt opened her heart to her niece and laid out the events of the last year. Carolyn talked for almost an hour. Emily, a born listener, quietly pondered what she was hearing. Finally, Carolyn's rendition stopped.

Emily remained silent for a long time. When she did speak, it was softly. "Do you think he loves you?"

Carolyn didn't want to answer the question. "I guess I'd say yes. But how can I trust him? How can I forgive him?"

Emily shook her head. "It may not be easy. I know that for a long time, every time I'd see Harriet Taylor, her nasty words would replay in my head. Every slight or sly comment or ugly thing she'd said about me would come to mind when I'd meet her. Given the size of Alderdale and Harriet's propensity to be out and about the town, I was feeling that way a lot. One day as I passed her, I realized my anger and hurt were hurting me but having no effect on her. She hadn't a clue I was upset with her." Emily paused and winked at Carolyn. "You know Harriet. She thought she'd been doing me favors all those years. I was the one still suffering."

Emily smiled softly. "I decided to do the thing I least wanted to do. I began to invite her to join Nathan and me for Sunday dinner. At first, I thought she'd refuse. You know, have much more important invitations for Sunday dinner. I was wrong. She accepted. She's been coming over to our house every Sunday. You know what I've learned? I think deep down, Harriet's meddling is a way she keeps herself busy. I don't think she is real fond of her own company. I know that since Amelia left, Harriet doesn't feel useful. She is a lonely woman. After I reached out and forgave her, I began to see her in a new light. She's still as meddlesome as can be, but she's kind of sad."

Emily's story reminded Carolyn of her recent visit with Herman Dobbs. Remembering her feelings of compassion for the desperate but highly annoying man, Carolyn said, "I see what you mean, but what does that have to do with Michael?"

Emily thought for a moment. "I guess what I'm trying to say

is, if we are focused on our own hurt and pain, sometimes we miss out on what is really there. It wasn't until I forgave Harriet that I could see her pain. It may not be until you forgive Michael that you can see how great his love is for you. I believe there is a reason God asks us to forgive one another. Part of it is for the other person, but I think most of it is for us."

Throughout the day and the remainder of Emily's visit, Carolyn thought about what Emily had said. Slowly she began to recognize the lesson. She had to forgive Michael, but it didn't stop there. She had to forgive Marti's family; she had to forgive Harriet—Queen Matchmaker; and she had to forgive the attorneys who fired her, as well. It wasn't about what any of them had done. It was about her. It was about what her reaction to them was doing to her.

After Emily left, Carolyn knelt down by her bed. She began by thanking her heavenly Father for her many blessings. Then she asked for His help in learning to forgive and move on. When she concluded her prayer, Carolyn found peace. She knew all would be well. Now she needed to tell Michael.

Michael's relief at hearing her voice after more than a week of silence was readily apparent. "Carolyn, I'm so glad you called."

Carolyn swallowed hard. "Well, Michael, I've got to tell you, I'm not real happy about you not being honest with me in the first place. You should have told me—regardless of what you thought my reaction would be." She paused, then continued. "However, I can understand how I may have made it a bit hard for you to tell me. I made it pretty clear what I thought about attorneys. I'm starting to work through that, though. I just wanted to let you know I forgive you."

Michael's joy leaked through the phone. "Hot dog! I thought I might have lost you. What changed your mind?"

"Your birthday present."

"I don't understand. . . ." Michael's voice echoed confusion.

"Emily. She reminded me what forgiveness was all about. Besides, how long could I stay mad at someone who sent my favorite niece to me on my seventieth birthday? I still can't figure out how you knew about her. I've only mentioned Emily to you once. How did you find her?"

Michael muttered something about trade secrets, then rapidly changed the subject. "Don't suppose you're up for some ice cream and a good walk. I'm in the mood to celebrate."

Carolyn replied, "I'm always up for ice cream, but what are we celebrating?"

Michael's response was soft. "I've just been reunited with the woman I love."

nineteen

Carolyn's lesson in forgiveness did not end with Michael. She wrote a letter in care of the hospital to Marti's brother and sister, apologizing for her interference and expressing her gratitude for the time she'd spent with Marti. She visited the hospital administration. Her appearance, coupled with glowing recommendations from Ruth and the charge nurse, Denise, landed her back as a Community Memorial volunteer. She even signed and sent back the waiver of litigation form the law firm had tried to get her to sign when they issued her severance package. Holding the sealed, addressed envelope, she comforted herself.

"Even if I'd been able to take them to the cleaners, it would have been more years that I would have had to interact with them. At my age, every year counts. Besides, after spending the majority of my life working on lawsuits, why on earth would I want to waste the rest of it doing the same thing?" Her self-motivational speech did the trick. The envelope was deposited in a U.S. mailbox within the hour.

Getting back into the volunteer routine was just what Carolyn's spirit needed. Between her weekly hospital duties and Michael's planned adventures, Carolyn sometimes wondered if she weren't as busy as she had been before "retiring."

Back on the Transitional Care Unit, Carolyn had the chance to meet a lot of seniors preparing to make the journey from the hospital back to their homes. She was able to help those who weren't as lucky to cope with the realization they'd be going to a nursing facility. Carolyn found that given the events of the last year, she was more than capable of understanding the devastation a major life change could bring. Her experience, though far different from the experiences of the seniors she was counseling, proved remarkably helpful in allowing her to relate. She also enjoyed making follow-up visits outside of her volunteer duties to her friends' new assisted-living abodes. Somehow, her frank assurances that they would survive seemed to provide comfort. Perhaps her forthright demeanor made them feel they had no choice but to take her word for it. Whatever the reason, Carolyn Sheffield found a new calling.

Even the nurses recognized her valuable contribution. They began assigning her to all patients who would not be returning to their own homes. In the spare moments Carolyn had left, she was delegated the mind-enriching duty of chart filing. On one of the rare occasions she was filing charts, Carolyn came across a familiar name—Michael Flannigan. Carolyn was confused. Why would Michael have a recent Transitional Care Unit chart? He hadn't said anything. Maybe it was a different Michael Flannigan.

The moral twinges of her conscience couldn't stand a chance against the years of ingrained investigative instinct. As she "accidentally" dropped the chart to the floor, it "fell open." Carolyn couldn't lift her gaze from the pages. Her throat dropped to her stomach. She was no medical genius, but even she knew what the words R/O hepatic CA stood for; the doctors thought Michael had cancer. Liver cancer. Carolyn couldn't even say good-bye to the hospital staff. She picked the chart off the floor, set it on the counter, and left for home.

For a week, Carolyn wrestled with what to do. She diligently avoided answering the phone. The doorbell rang with no response. Memories of Marti flooded back. Carolyn's intense struggle permeated every aspect of her life. She didn't sleep. She couldn't eat. Her infamous postfiring hairdo threatened to make a curtain call. No matter how she played it out in her head, the solution seemed unavoidable. Much as she loved Michael Flannigan, and her restless nights had left no question that she did, she couldn't risk giving her heart to him if he was going to die. She couldn't face the hurt again. Finally resolute, but devastated in her decision, Carolyn made the call.

"Michael?"

His relief was instantly apparent. "Carolyn? Are you okay? I've been so worried. I've called. I've rung your doorbell. No one answered. Even Ruth didn't know where you were. Are you sick? Do you need help? I can't tell you how concerned I've been."

Michael's reaction made what Carolyn had to do even harder. "Michael, I know everything. I know about the cancer. I know you could die. I can't go through another death of someone I love. I lost Marti. Hard as that was, it wouldn't even start to compare with losing you. I'm sorry. I thought I was strong, but I'm not. I don't have a choice. I love you, but our relationship has to end."

Michael's silence spoke volumes. Finally, Carolyn heard his voice.

"I probably know better than anyone else, Carolyn, that when you set your mind to something, you aren't real open to changing it. I can tell you, however, that even though I felt like I'd died inside after I lost Elise, I wouldn't exchange the time I had with her for anything. There are no guarantees in this life, but I love you. Even if you don't want to listen to my pleadings, at least promise me you'll pray about it."

Willing to say anything to be released from the uncomfortable conversation, Carolyn gave her word.

The sad good-bye haunted Carolyn in the lonely autumn weeks that followed. Each twinge of regret was met with an equally strong twinge of relief that she would not risk the full emotional brunt of Michael's death. Despite her attempts to put on a strong front and reclaim her "terminally single and proud of it" mantra, Carolyn couldn't find the old gumption to put behind it.

Now that her days weren't filled with exciting adventure, Carolyn had more time to spend with Ruth. Despite the curiosity that oozed from Ruth's pores, she didn't say one word about Michael. Ruth's matchmaking prowess had its limits, and her silence showed she knew better than to touch her friend's freshly opened wounds. Carolyn found comfort in Ruth's presence. In lifelong friendship there was a constancy that soothed life's roughest spots.

"So how is your work going in the TCU? You still bringing your boot camp bedside manner to those seniors?" Ruth joked one day at lunch.

Carolyn ruefully rolled her eyes. "You know the funny thing? Those of us who have lived this many years seem to have an understanding. Even if we don't speak the same language, or in the same manner, there is something about a caring heart that seems to provide the translation. I think some of the younger folks feel that the only reason the older generation listens to me is because I'm an old battle-axe who won't take any guff. They're wrong. I believe they listen to me because the lines in my face show them my assurances that they will make it through these tough times are based on experience. And in this life there is nothing quite like having someone who has been there to hold your hand."

"Amen to that, sister," Ruth added. "I'll tell you, after my husband, Jim, died, I wouldn't have made it through without my support group. Sometimes one of us would start a sentence about how we were feeling, and the whole group could finish it. We had arrived from all different walks of life, but our one shared experience in losing a spouse provided an instant bond."

Carolyn couldn't help but ask, "Do you still miss him? Like burning, aching in your gut miss him?"

Ruth removed her glasses. "Oh, yes. He's been gone a decade, and I still wake up in the middle of the night and roll over to put my arms around him. A couple of times I've trailed old men around the grocery store believing they might be my Jim. Good thing I don't look more sinister, or I might have a couple of stalking charges around my neck. I miss him terribly. Sometimes so much that I pray I might just feel his presence for another minute. Every time I wish upon a star, I pray for one more day with my husband. I know it will never come true, but I can always hope."

"Would you wish for another day even if you knew you'd lose him and have to face the pain again after it ended?" Carolyn asked.

"You better believe it," Ruth insisted. "See, that's the thing about real love. Even a minute of it makes your life better."

Ruth and Carolyn finished their open-faced sandwiches and said their good-byes. Yet late into the night, Carolyn pondered her friend's words. Was love really that powerful? Was it really worth risking everything? Suddenly she remembered her vow to Michael. She had told him she'd pray about it. So it was a few weeks late—she could still live up to her promise.

She knelt and laid out her concerns to her heavenly Father. When she finished, a verse she had learned long ago in Sunday school, Proverbs 3:5–6, came into her head: "Trust in the LORD with all thine heart; and lean not unto thine own understanding. In all thy ways acknowledge him, and he shall direct thy paths."

Ruth didn't have any minutes left with Jim. Carolyn did have time left with Michael. She wasn't sure how long or what the outcome would be, but she knew however long it was, her life would be better because of it.

This phone call was much easier to make than the one she had made a few weeks earlier. "Michael?"

"Carolyn?" Michael spoke only her name.

"You know I'm not one who readily admits she's wrong. Of course, it's probably because I have to do it so infrequently." Carolyn chuckled in her nervousness.

This time it was Michael who came to the point. "Carolyn, break it to me. 'Forward and Direct,' that's my motto. Or at least it's the motto of a good friend of mine."

Michael's lighthearted reference to the words she so often muttered released Carolyn's voice. "I just realized that each day I don't see you is one less day I have to put you in your place. I don't know how long you'll have; maybe it'll turn out you don't even have cancer. Then again, I don't know how long I'll have. Given my emotional state this last year, I'm beginning to wonder if something is wrong with me, too. I guess I'm trying to say you're stuck with me. That is, if you still want me."

"Still want you?" Michael's voice shook. "Where else would I find someone who can conduct herself as admirably at a good old-fashioned, husband dressing-down? You better believe I still want you."

❧

December 1 brought a layer of snow to Seattle. Carolyn awoke and donned a cream-colored sweater set. It was going to be a cold day. She poured herself a mug of hot chocolate and relaxed back into the familiar grasp of her living-room couch. The sound of sleigh bells brought her to her feet. She moved toward the door to answer the knock. Standing clad in a long gray wool coat and cream scarf, Michael looked as dapper as a magazine advertisement. In the background Carolyn could see a carriage drawn by two horses and complete with driver.

"Get on your coat, my dear. We're going for a ride," Michael invited.

He didn't have to extend the invitation twice. Carolyn pulled on a long red wool coat, a matching hat, and mittens. She was going on a sleigh ride. When she got in, she gasped.

Gerbera daisies lined the carriage.

"How did you know? How did you get them at this time of year?" Carolyn queried.

Michael's response was a bit hesitant. "Well, the answer to the first question is kind of a long story."

"Go ahead," Carolyn urged.

"You see, when I was first going through all the tests to determine if I had cancer, they placed me in the Transitional Care Unit. Bed 122."

"Bed 122? That was right next to Marti. But I never saw you." Carolyn felt perplexed.

"I was pretty sick. And on the other side of the curtain. I didn't see you, either. But I heard you. I didn't put two and two together until you started talking about Marti. I realized the deeply intelligent, sensitive woman I was hearing was the same woman who gave me the biggest what-for I'd ever had coming to me." Michael paused, taking Carolyn's hand. "I wanted to tell you, but when you opened up with me on your own, there didn't seem to be a huge need. After I started spending time with you, I got to see the sensitive woman firsthand. I didn't just hear her through a sheet. I did, however, get a few interesting tidbits of information."

"The gerbera daisy bouquet." Carolyn suddenly remembered. "If you knew how many hours I spent trying to figure out who sent that! And the orange creams from See's. Nobody knew about them. So that's how you found out! The new journal! You must have seen mine in Marti's room. You wanted me to have one." One by one the pieces fell into place. "And *that's* how you knew about Emily. You heard me tell Marti about her."

Carolyn fell into shocked silence.

"All true, my dear." Michael took her other hand and knelt down on the narrow carriage floor. "But it was inadvertent and certainly not purposeful. Besides, didn't you get some great gifts out of it? Gerbera daisies. Orange creams. Emily at Christmas. I promise, no more secrets—but there's one condition."

Carolyn looked at him warily. "I am not fond of conditions."

Michael looked up from his kneeling position. "I think you might like this one. No more secrets, but you have to agree to be my wife."

Carolyn was shocked but recovered quickly. Uncharacteristically planting a kiss on his forehead, she responded, "You got it. But only as long as the See's orange creams and gerbera daisies keep coming."

As Michael smiled, Carolyn silently thanked God she had found "Christmas" in the winter of her life.

epilogue

Alderdale, Oregon, December 30

The whisper of furtive footsteps, the rustle of clothing, and the heavy scent of perfume accompanied the first guest to enter the evergreen wreathed, white-light-adorned reception hall of the small church in which Carolyn Sheffield had just become Mrs. Michael Flannigan.

Harriet Taylor slowly scanned the beautifully decorated room and smiled with satisfaction. No one could ever say Alderdale didn't care for its own. Although Carolyn Sheffield had left the village almost fifty years earlier, the townsfolk had turned out en masse for her wedding.

A murmur in the hall leading from the chapel replaced caution with haste. Straight to the front of the reception room she strode, the carpet mercifully muffling her steps. Once there, she carefully scrutinized the name cards on the head table. She had not been included among the most favored. Instead, a card bearing her name mocked her from an adjacent table.

Harriet glared at the last two cards at the end of the head table: *Ms. Denise Thornton, Mr. Bob Marin.* "Well!" she exclaimed. "I'll just see about that. As sure as my name is Harriet Taylor, Ms. Denise Thornton, whoever she is, is *not* going to sit at the head table. After all, I'm family."

The laughter and voices in the hall grew louder. In another moment, the wedding party would burst into the room. Harriet set her jaw and grimly snatched the offensive bit of pasteboard with one hand, her own name card with the other.

166

A lightning exchange worthy of one skilled in the fine art of sleight of hand relegated the unknown woman to the place of lesser importance, leaving the last two cards at the end of the table to read *Mr. Bob Marin* and *Mrs. Harriet Taylor*.

With a purr of accomplishment, Harriet fled from the table just before the wedding party entered and planted herself in prime position to be first in the reception line.

➣

Carolyn Sheffield Flannigan glanced at the sleeve of the classic cream silk suit embroidered with pearls that she had chosen for her wedding day. The small pearls glistened, but not as brightly as the two pearls flanking the large diamond on her ring finger. She entwined her fingers with Michael's.

He glanced down at her. "Lovely wedding."

"Yes. It's a good thing. It's the only one I plan to have."

His hearty laugh rang out. "It better be. Besides, a man like me only comes along once every seventy years. You better hold on to me while you have the chance. Now smile and greet our well-wishers."

Carolyn grinned at him. "Look who's first. What a surprise." She gestured toward the tall, spare woman in a dark blue dress, obviously purchased for the occasion, who was sailing toward them full steam ahead, and beaming like a lighthouse. "Harriet Taylor, in person."

"Oh, the lady Bob Marin admires."

Carolyn bit her tongue to hold back a sharp reply. No way would she mar her wedding day with a recitation of all the reasons Bob should *not* admire Harriet.

After greeting Emily and Nathan Hamilton, Harriet reached her target. "Dear Carolyn," she gushed. "I am thrilled for you. I just knew someday you would find love and happiness." She shook the groom's hand as if it were a pump handle. "Mr. Flannigan. I hope you know just how lucky you are to capture our dear Carolyn's heart."

"I certainly do."

Carolyn heard the current of laughter just beneath the surface of Michael's heartfelt reply. She felt her lips twitch. Harriet was Harriet, and perhaps—as Emily had said—the woman's meddling came from loneliness.

Harriet leaned forward. For once in her life, she had the courtesy to lower her voice before saying, "Carolyn, I want to thank you so much for what you did for Herman."

Carolyn stiffened. "Herman? You mean Herman Dobbs?"

"Oh, yes." Harriet rushed on. "Herman took your advice and signed up for a cooking class." She smiled broadly. "It won't surprise me one bit if he finds himself a wife there. He says a couple of very eligible ladies are enrolled." She threw a smile at Bob Marin, who stood beside Michael. "So many weddings. Love is certainly in the Alderdale air; don't you agree, Mr. Marin?"

Carolyn lost Bob's reply in Emily's giggle. "Hush," she ordered her niece, whose face was as crimson, from trying to hold back laughter, as the floor length gown that so became her. "If you get me started, I'll never stop. Oh, Isaiah. Mrs. Gerard. Good to see you. Have you met my friend Ruth Welch?" She nodded toward the white-haired friend in the gorgeous scarlet gown who was vainly attempting to shepherd people through the reception line and to their places at the tables.

"We have," the attorney boomed. "Charming lady. Congratulations, Flannigan."

A tug on Carolyn's arm, followed by a gasp during a slight lull in the greetings, turned the bride's attention back to Emily. "Aunt Carolyn, did you change the cards on the head table? I thought you placed your nurse friend Denise, from the hospital where you volunteer, next to Bob Marin."

"I did. Why—what on earth. . . ?" Carolyn stared at the angular woman taking her place at the end of the table and smiling at Bob Marin as if her dearest wish had been granted.

"Harriet at the head table? How? When?"

"Who knows?" A ripple of laughter from Emily subsided, and she said, "Let it go, Aunt Carolyn. In all the years I've known Harriet, I've never seen her look happier."

Carolyn's mounting irritation subsided. "I guess if it means that much to her to sit at the head table next to Bob Marin, it's all right, even if she did perform some hocus-pocus to get there."

She didn't realize Michael had overheard the conversation until he quietly said, "Boy, she is a bit of a manipulator, isn't she? But she does appear to be happy. And Bob is obviously enjoying your friend's company."

Carolyn rolled her eyes at Harriet's typical antics. In another hour or two, she would part company with Harriet. Even two more hours with Harriet Taylor didn't seem too daunting on her wedding day, especially with Michael by her side. In the meantime, a delicious meal catered by a high-end Portland deli awaited them.

≈

If Carolyn believed her wedding would be free from any further Harriet-style shenanigans, she was sorely mistaken.

The tasty meal and good wishes lasted long into the afternoon. All that remained was for Carolyn to throw her bouquet, then begin her new life as Carolyn Sheffield Flannigan. Mrs. Michael Flannigan.

"Throw your bouquet, my dear," Michael urged. "We need to be on our way."

The look of love and quick way he squeezed her hand warmed Carolyn. They stepped out of the church. A light snow the night before had frosted shrubs and trees, but roads and sidewalks soon dried. Now the late afternoon sunlight pouring down on Alderdale turned it into a wonderland as sparkling as the cider with which the wedding toasts had been given.

Carolyn paused on the steps, remembering Emily's wedding

and the laughter that swept through the crowd when she caught her niece's bouquet. How inappropriate and unwanted it had seemed at the time. Yet God had known her future—and Michael's. A phrase from the wedding ceremony came to mind. . ."*as long as you both shall live.*" She glanced at Michael and silently thanked her heavenly Father.

"Ready?" Michael prodded. "Close your eyes and let 'em fly."

Carolyn smiled and shut her eyes.

"Wait for me," a familiar voice called.

Carolyn's eyes popped back open. Face avid and flushed with exertion, Harriet Taylor pushed through the group of girls and women intent on catching the prize.

Carolyn choked back a laugh and flung the flowers. Up, up, then down they arched. With a triumphant cry, Harriet sharply elbowed aside three smaller women, outreached the others, and snatched the bouquet.

The joy in her face when she cradled the flowers in her bony arms and searched the crowd to find an applauding Bob Marin, actually brought a lump to Carolyn's throat. Filled with her own happiness, she quickly shot a prayer skyward, a prayer that Ms. Harriet Taylor, second cousin thrice removed—or whatever she was—might find some of the happiness God had bestowed on Michael and her.

Carolyn smiled at her husband and stepped into their car. She cast a farewell look at Ruth and Emily, and the radiance in their faces warmed her like a benediction. She raised her arm in farewell, then turned her gaze to the beckoning, ice-touched, tree-lined road. A road she knew from experience held many twists and bends. A road she and Michael would travel together, for as long as God in His wisdom permitted.

A Letter To Our Readers

Dear Reader:

In order that we might better contribute to your reading enjoyment, we would appreciate your taking a few minutes to respond to the following questions. We welcome your comments and read each form and letter we receive. When completed, please return to the following:

Fiction Editor
Heartsong Presents
PO Box 719
Uhrichsville, Ohio 44683

1. Did you enjoy reading *Changing Seasons* by Colleen L. Reece and Renee DeMarco?
   ❏ Very much! I would like to see more books by this author!
   ❏ Moderately. I would have enjoyed it more if

   _____

   _____

   _____

2. Are you a member of **Heartsong Presents**? ❏ Yes ❏ No
   If no, where did you purchase this book? _____

   _____

3. How would you rate, on a scale from 1 (poor) to 5 (superior), the cover design? _____

4. On a scale from 1 (poor) to 10 (superior), please rate the following elements.

   ____ Heroine   ____ Plot
   ____ Hero   ____ Inspirational theme
   ____ Setting   ____ Secondary characters

5. These characters were special because? _____
   _____
   _____

6. How has this book inspired your life? _____
   _____
   _____

7. What settings would you like to see covered in future
   Heartsong Presents books? _____
   _____
   _____

8. What are some inspirational themes you would like to see
   treated in future books? _____
   _____
   _____

9. Would you be interested in reading other **Heartsong
   Presents** titles? ❑ Yes ❑ No

10. Please check your age range:
     ❑ Under 18   ❑ 18-24
     ❑ 25-34   ❑ 35-45
     ❑ 46-55   ❑ Over 55

Name _____
Occupation _____
Address _____
City_____ State_____ Zip_____

Texas
Charm

4 stories in 1

Love is in the air around Houston as told in four complete novels by DiAnn Mills. Four contemporary Texas women seek life's charm amid some of its deepest pain—such as broken relationships and regrets of the past.

Contemporary, paperback, 480 pages, 5 ³/₁₆"x 8"

Presents